Published in United States
By Erin M Munn, Quincy, MA

ISBN 9781482379662

Manufactured in United States
First edition published 2013
Cover art and jacket designed © 2013 (by) Erin M Munn

Realizing Mr. Right

Erin M Munn

Thank you to Julie, Tom and Kate for always being my cheerleaders and helping me realize my dreams. Thank you to all who have supported me through my life, I couldn't have done this without you.

Thank you!!

Contents

CHAPTER ONE

I thought about starting this book where we begin at a wedding and then do the whole lets work backwards until we find out who the groom is and how they got here. But the story doesn't really warrant that. To anyone from the outside looking in, or just anyone that wasn't me, the who, becomes obvious quickly, I guess it's the how that we should address. But it is important to start from the beginning.

When I was twelve, I had a best friend named Allison Jacobs, Allie. We met the first day of seventh grade. I was new in school and some girls were giving me a hard time at lunch. Allie 'accidentally' spilled her soda on one of the girls and then smiled at me. That's how it was with the two of us, always protecting one another from any harm we could control. We found out we had the same favorite movies, and we liked the same music she became my best friend almost instantly, and as time went on she became like a sister to me. She had a younger brother named Brandon who used to enjoy annoying us. He was three years younger; just nine when we became friends and the deepness of New Kids on the Block lyrics seemed to escape him. He was a thorn in our side that we simply tolerated for about six years.

I never thought of him as anything more than a little brother. That was until Allie and I were having our last girl's night before leaving for college. She was going to California and I was staying in Massachusetts going to photography school. We were sitting on the couch watching 16 candles for possibly the 300th time and talking about how often we would be visiting each other, when Brandon came home. It was the first time I had seen him since school had ended. He had just turned 15 and made the varsity lacrosse team so he was away at camp all summer.

When he walked into the room, his appearance caught me off guard. He looked like he had grown about a foot since the last time I had seen him, although it was more likely that I just hadn't been paying attention. He was about six feet tall now, his dark brown, almost black hair was cut very short, and his chocolate brown eyes almost sparkled when he looked at me. The combination of his mother being a quarter Cherokee and the exposure to the sun had turned his skin the most amazing shade of bronze and made his smile that much more dazzling. He left the room again not having said anything to us.

"Holy Crap!" I whispered, however not soft enough to escape Allie's attention.

She laughed, "Um gross. That's my bother." She said pushing me slightly.

I looked at her and shook my head. "No honey that beautiful creature cannot be your brother, that is..."

She interrupted me. "He will be very happy to know you think so." She laughed and I looked away.

"What the hell was that?" I thought to myself, "He's still Brandon. Who cares if he is suddenly beautiful?" I shrugged and we went back to talking.

"Hey Ladies," Brandon said coming back into the room. He plopped himself down on the floor beside me. I could only imagine the ridiculous look I had on my face. He smiled widely at me. "Emma," he said nudging me, "you ok? You look even whiter than usual." He looked slightly concerned which made Allie laugh and my face flush.

"No I'm fine," I said in almost a whisper. His close proximity to me was suddenly making me nervous. "Still the same kid, still the same kid," I kept repeating in my head.

"You need to get some sun girl; you're the only person I know who stays the color of Elmer's glue all year long." He laughed.

"I tan," I said. They looked at each other and both raised an eyebrow at me. "What? I do." I insisted.

"Yes dear," Allie started "you turn a lovely shade of off white" and they both laughed.

"Oh fuck you guys," I said crossing my arms over my chest, "I come from a long line of pasty people." I pouted trying to fight a smile.

"Awe my poor little pasty girl" Brandon said wrapping his arms around me and giving me a hug. His possessive word only vaguely escaped me.

His hug sent and electrical surge though my body so intense that I shook. He pulled back and looked at my face. I smiled sheepishly at him and giggled. "Very bazaar," I thought to myself.

Allie rolled her eyes at me, but she smiled. He kept his arm around me as we sat and talked. After a few hours Allie laid down on the floor against a couch pillow. I started to do the same but Brandon pulled me into him so my head was resting against his inner shoulder. I looked at him puzzled, but he just smiled at me. When I turned back around Allie was asleep.

I turned and looked at Brandon and then his arm around me and then back to his face with a questioning look. He laughed, "Well I hugged you because you looked like you needed one, and then, well my arm just sort of stayed around you. It felt kind of nice." He said turning away and smiling shyly. "So when you didn't ask me to move it, well I was glad, so I just kept it there." He shrugged and I just nodded at him and smiled. "So um…"

"What?" I asked, still trying to wrap my head around why it was I didn't ask him to move his arm when he asked that exact question.

"Why didn't you make me move my arm?" He looked down when he asked but when he looked back at me his eyes were soft and sweet, I smiled at him. "Not that I'm complaining." He grinned.

"I have no idea." I admitted giggling. "I just um…" I stopped for a second. He was staring at me, waiting for an answer. "I just didn't want you to move it I guess. I was comfortable. Weird right?" I asked and smiled.

His return smile was triumphant and slightly smug. "I would expect nothing less than weird from you." He teased. "So do I look all grown up now?" he said motioning to himself with his free hand. I just giggled and rolled my eyes. "I will take that as a yes." He said grinning at me. "You know Emm; you're the most beautiful girl I have ever known, inside and out."

I could feel myself blushing. "You're still young." I said

He shook his head, an annoyed look on his face, "nothing to do with it." He said. "You know the way you looked at me when I came in the door, like you were seeing me for the first time." I looked away embarrassed at my obvious pleasure in his new appearance. He smiled, "I had to leave the room to compose myself. I have been waiting a long time to see the look from you."

I just stared at him, I couldn't do anything else. This was the most surreal conversation and one I never planned to ever have with him, no matter how beautiful he was. Of course I hadn't been expecting that either. "Brandon I…." I was stopped mid sentence by his lips on mine, his free hand moved to caress my cheek. I thought about stopping him, about saying that this was insane and he was like my brother, but his kiss sent almost a shock through me and I couldn't stop him, I just kissed him back.

When he stopped he still held my face in his hands, inspecting it for any sign of anger, when he saw none he grinned. "I know that this may be the only time in my life I ever get to kiss you. I'm sorry I just couldn't pass up my one chance." He smiled his most sweet smile and I couldn't help but giggle. "So how'd I do?" he asked.

"Eh." I said but I couldn't stop myself from grinning. "Not bad for a fifteen year old" I said winking at him.

He pretended to be dejected. "I thought it was pretty good." He said confidently. I laughed, "Oh well I better try again then." Before I could speak he kissed me again, making my head spin, his hands reached for my hair pulling me closer. It was amazing and I didn't want him to stop. "Better?" he asked when he finally pulled away. I held up one finger to him not able to speak. He laughed. "And I will take that as a yes too."

I laughed and then became serious. "Brandon, I…" I tried to start again, remembering what I had intended to say to him before his lips scrambled my brain.

He stopped me again. "I know," he said smiling; it was a sadder smile now. "Aside from the fact that you're leaving for school, I am too young for you right now." I nodded he pulled me close and kissed my head. "That's ok, like I said; I never thought I would get the chance to do that. Now I have, twice, so I'm happy." He kissed my head again, pulling me closer and closing his eyes.

"You can come visit me at school if you want" I said smiling.

He opened his eyes and looked at me, "really?" he asked with a smirk.

"Yeah, I think I would like that. But as friends only."

"I can deal with that." He said smiling and closing his eyes again. A few days later Allie and I both left for school.

CHAPTER TWO

About two weeks into the semester there was a knock on my door. "Strange." I thought and got up to answer it.

When I opened it Brandon was standing there with a big goofy grin on his face, "hey Emm." He said

"Brandon," I said shocked.

"I'm sorry, I guess I should have called, but you told me I could come visit you at school so I thought." But he stopped himself and smiled at me again.

I laughed, "Its ok Hun, what's up? And how did you get here?"

"My dad dropped me off, I have something for you."

"You do?"

He ginned, "I got these." He said and pulled two tickets from his pocket.

"Are those what I think they are?" I said smiling and starting to bounce up and down. He was holding two red sox tickets in his hand.

He chuckled and nodded, "I waited outside for like four hours. I skipped school, my mom wasn't happy but when I told her that they were for you, she seemed to almost be ok with it."

I laughed, "Well thank you. When is the game?"

"Um...tonight" he said and grinned.

"Ok" I said and grabbed my coat, "let's go."

"Emma, its noon, the game doesn't start until seven."

I looked at him and smiled, "it will take us an hour to get back to Quincy, and then we have to take the train in and sit in the stadium and just be."

"Just be what?"

"Just be there, Fenway is my happy place."

He laughed at me and we left. The whole way back to Quincy he told me about school. He told me about all of the girls in his class, but that he wasn't dating any of them. When I asked why he just laughed and said that they just didn't interest him like some other girls did. I thought it was best at that point to drop the discussion of girls, plus I was a bit more jealous than I had expected to be.

When we finally got to the park he turned to me, "thanks for coming with me Emma Grace."

I turned and looked at him strangely, "why did you call me that?" I asked, "oh and thank you for asking me." I smiled.

"I don't know I like the way it sounds." He said "do you not like it?"

I thought about it for a minute, "No I think I like it."

"Oh good, cause I wasn't planning on stopping." He chuckled and we walked into the park.

The game was great, we had some hot dogs and some overpriced soda. The whole time we were sitting next to one another I felt like my arm was on fire. I was trying to stop myself from touching him but around the seventh inning I had no choice, he put his arm around me. I could feel my body shaking. "You ok?" he asked with a chuckle.

I just looked at him and laughed, "Yeah, I'm fine." I said, but I wasn't entirely sure it was true.

"Are you cold?"

"No, I'm just..." I turned and looked at him, "I just feel a little weird."

"It's my male magnetism isn't it?" he chuckled. I just rolled my eyes at him.

"Brandon you know..." I said looking at him seriously.

"Emma, I am perfectly happy just being your friend, if I am ever meant to be anything more than I will be, but until then, I am more than ok with just this."

"Seriously awkward moments and strange electricity that doesn't seem to make any sense?"

He chuckled again, "yes all that is lovely in my eyes." I smiled at him.

"You're a good man Brandon."

"Man?"

"I thought it would sound a bit condescending if I called you a boy." I giggled.

He rolled his eyes and kissed my forehead. "You're a beautiful person Emma Grace. I am glad I get the chance to be your friend."

"Are you sure you're only fifteen?" I asked him with a giggle.

"I wish every moment I was with you that I wasn't." he said with a sheepish smile.

I laughed and wrapped my arm through his as we started to make our way through the crowd to the T.

"I had a really good time tonight" he said when we were almost home.

"So did I," I said and then giggled at the surprise in my voice. He laughed and then put his arm around me. "I like being your friend, your sister would never come to a game with me."

"You can always count on me to be your Fenway buddy." He said with a laugh.

"That's good to know."

"Can I come see you again, even if I don't have tickets to a game?"

I smiled and laughed, "Yes, I think that would be great. I am sorry it took me so long to see what a great guy you are, your fun you know. Your funny too, that was a surprise."

"You're just easily amused." He said chuckling.

"That's true, but you're still funny." I pulled up in front of his house and stopped the car.

"Are you going back to school now?" he asked

"I think I might go home and hang out with my parents. I might go back tomorrow."

He nodded, "you want to have breakfast in the morning?' he asked looking away, "just as friends of course."

I laughed, "I would love to have breakfast with you, and I'll pick you up around ten."

"Excellent!" he said with more enthusiasm than even he expected. He chuckled, "um… ok I'm going to go then." He opened the car door.

"Brandon," I said and he turned to look at me, "good night." I said and kissed his cheek. He blushed.

"Good night Emma Grace, see you in the morning." and he got out.

We went to breakfast the next morning and then I went back to school. I talked to him almost as much as I talked to his sister. He would send me an e-mail just about every day and call me about once a week. We were becoming great friends; in fact I could honestly say he was quickly becoming one of my very best friends.

CHAPTER THREE

6 months later, the night before I was heading home to meet Allie so we could go to spring break in Hawaii, I got a phone call from Allie and Brandon's mother.

"Hello?" I said groggily. It was about three in the morning.

"Emma?" she said.

"Mrs. Jacobs?" I said snapping awake immediately. Why could she possibly be calling me? Was Allie ok, was Brandon. "What's the matter? What's wrong?"

"Emma sweetheart, it's your mom and dad. I… I think you should come home dear. There's been an accident."

"What? What kind of accident?"

"Honey Steve and Brandon are coming to get you."

"What happened Lorraine? Are my parents ok?"

"Emma sweetie, you parents were in a car accident tonight. They were hit by a drunk driver."

"Are they ok?"She paused; I could hear both the fear and sadness in her voice. Our parents had grown to be best friends through our friendship. I knew that whatever she had to tell me was hard enough that she couldn't just say it. "They didn't make it did they?" I asked.

"Oh Emma I'm so sorry."

"I have to go." I was stunned. I couldn't think straight. All I knew was I needed to get home.

"Emma honey, wait."

"I have to go home."

"The boys are coming to get you."

"Who?" I asked. Nothing seemed to be making any sense. Suddenly there was a knock at the door. "There's someone here, I have to go." And I hung up on her. Completely dazed I got up and walked to the door. When I opened it Brandon and his father were standing there. Suddenly the impact of what Lorraine had just said hit me and I fell to the ground sobbing.

"Emma!" I heard someone say and then I was in a fog after that. I remember Brandon helping me up and sitting on my bed while his father grabbed the bags I had packed for my trip. And I vaguely remember the ride home sitting in the back seat all while Brandon never let go of me. He didn't speak, at least not that I can remember. He just held me until we got back to his house. When we stopped in his drive way his mother came running out to the car. I looked around at all of them.

"I have to go home." I said. I suddenly needed to occupy my mind as much as possible. It was about 7 am now and my head was still fuzzy, half from exhaustion and the other half from what I can only assume was trauma. They all looked at me worried. "There's a lot to do, I have a lot to do, and I have to go home." I kept saying to no one in particular.

"Emma, we can do all that later, I think you need some sleep sweetheart. Why don't you come in and just rest." Lorraine said. She came to give me a hug, but I could not seem to let go of her son, or he couldn't seem to let go of me. The details of a lot of it are still fuzzy.

I looked up at her and shook my head. "No, no I'm fine I just want to go home. I need… I need to go home." I looked up at Brandon. "Please take me home?" I said it like a question.

He looked back and forth between his parents. "I'll stay with her. Maybe she just needs…" they both nodded.

"I'll drive you." Steve said

"No," I started, "I think I need to walk. It's not far. Do you mind walking?" I looked up at Brandon. He smiled gently and shook his head. "Good" I said and took his hand and started walking. I could hear Lorraine's faint sobs as we walked.

"Um… Emma." He started when we had walked two of the four blocks to my house.

"Hmm?"

"Um…"

"I am waiting for it to sink in I think." I said to him. He nodded. "I just feel like I need to go home." He nodded again. "Thank you for coming with me. I know I don't deserve you being so good to me."

"I don't want to start a fight with you right now, but why would you ever say that. How can you believe that you have ever been anything less than amazing?"

"I'm too tired to fight back." I said smiling for what felt like the first time in forever. "Thank you." I said and leaned into his side as we walked up the front steps to my house. "Allie!" I said suddenly and looked up at him.

He smiled down at me. "She will be here tonight. I'll stay with you until then if you want." I nodded and wrapped my arms around his waist while he opened the front door.

When we walked into the house something inside me turned on. I went into practical mode. "Ok" I started, "if you're tired you are more than welcome to sit down and take a nap." I said as I started to climb the stairs.

"Where are you going?" he asked confused.

"There is a lot to do. I am going to have to go to the funeral home later, and I need to find clothes for them and I need to call for food."

"Emma," he started looking at me worried.

"If my brain is busy I can deal with it better." I looked at him and half smiled. "If I focus on the things that need to be done then I don't have to think about that fact that the two people I love most in the world are dead." I shrugged.

He came up the stairs and hugged me tightly. "I'll help you." he said. He took my hand and we walked up the stairs. We spent the next hour trying to find something to bring to the funeral home for my parents to wear. Then we called a few places about food; I just wanted to get some prices before everything was finalized. Through all of this Brandon never left my side.

About eleven in the morning his parents came to pick us up to take me to the funeral home to talk to the director about the arrangements. When everything was decided, the wake would be that following Monday and the funeral would be Tuesday. I finalized the rest of the arrangements, food and phone calls to their friends, we didn't have any family left to speak of. We drove to the airport to pick up Allie. The whole day Brandon was amazing and he held my hand.

When we were waiting in the baggage claim area for her, the weight of the day began to hit me. I leaned against Brandon to keep myself from falling over. He put his arm around me and kissed the top of my head. "You can sleep you know." He started, "you don't have to do everything, and you can let other people take care of you."

I smiled at him, "When did you get to be such a great guy? You're a really good friend Brandon."

"Hmm, ok I'll take that." He smiled at me. I smiled back at him and then closed my eyes.

I was asleep for what felt like hours; I woke up with a start, "Allie!" I said.

I could feel my body shaking from Brandon's chuckling beside me. "Hi sleepy head, you were only out for twenty minutes she's still de-boarding."

"Oh," I said embarrassed and blushed.

"How are you doing kid?" Steve asked.

I shrugged, "as good as I can be I guess. I still don't think it's really hit me though."

"You're doing fantastic." Lorraine said taking my hand.

"You're doing well yourself." I said. Her dark eyes were red from crying. It was clear that losing my mother, her best friend, was harder than she was trying to let me see. "You can be sad in front of me you know." I said. "Actually it might make it easier for me then I can remember how much everyone loved them. Protecting me isn't going to make dealing with it any easier when it finally sets in that they are gone."

Everyone looked at me and I suddenly felt awkward, so I just smiled. Then I heard someone call my name from across the crowded baggage claim.

"Emma!!!" I looked up and Allie was running across the room with her arms out stretched. I stood up and ran towards her. When we finally, what can only be described as collided she wrapped her arms around me and I started to sob, deep heaving sobs and once it started I didn't think it would ever stop. It was either her presence here or just the way she looked at me that it finally sank in that I was never going to see my parents again. She just hugged me and said, "Its ok, its ok." I knew she didn't mean that it was going to be ok, even though I am sure deep down I knew it would be some day, but she meant it was ok for me to cry. She knew me better than I almost knew myself.

.

Allie's parents went and got her luggage as she just stood there holding me as a sobbed. Poor Brandon stood there helpless looking lost, like he felt useless. When her luggage had been gathered and we were ready to leave I still had not stopped crying, before I knew what was going on, I felt like I was floating. When I opened my eyes Brandon was carrying me to the car. I felt a sudden twinge of electricity, which seemed to snap me out of my anguish momentarily. I looked up at his face and he smiled at me. "I'm too heavy for you to carry, I can walk." I said in between sobs.

He chuckled gently. "You're not heavy at all, and I don't think walking is something you would be very good at right now. For my own peace of mind can you please just let me do something?"

I realized he was right and I wasn't in any shape to take care of myself at the moment. I wrapped my arms around his neck and rested my head on his shoulder. "You smell good." I said and then giggled. He chuckled and then rolled his eyes at me. "Hey I am trying to focus on something good here."

"Sure, sure" he said chuckling again.

"Go to sleep." Allie said and pats me on the head. I tried to rebel but I was completely exhausted and I fell asleep before we even made it to the car. How they got me in the car I still don't know.

When I finally woke up I was in Allie's enormous bed with a Jacobs asleep on either side of me. I could see from her alarm clock that it was about two in the morning. I sighed at how awake I suddenly was and Allie opened her eyes.

"Hi sunshine," She said

I smiled weakly at her, "howdy" I answered.

She wrapped her arms around me and kissed my fore head. "I'm here buddy; I'll help you get through this. We both will." She motioned to her sleeping brother on my other side who was snoring quietly. "Has he done a good job in my absence?" she asked

"He's a good boy. I couldn't ask for a better second family that's for sure."

"We Love you Emm. We are going to get you through this the best we can."

CHAPTER FOUR

Sunday was probably the hardest day. Everything was already planned so I had nothing really to focus on. I made lists, I like lists they help me focus, list of all the things that needed to be done to put my parents affairs in order. Planning what to do with my parent's clothes and cars and house was not something I ever thought that I would have to deal with at the age of eighteen, but you have to go with the hand that life deals you.

"You don't have to figure it all out now you know." Brandon said sitting down beside me and looking at what I was writing.

I smiled at him, "I know it makes me feel better to be organized with things like this. If I know what I have to do then I won't leave anything out."

He shook his head at me and smiled. "If you need help with anything you know I am around."

"I do, thank you Hun." I smiled at him again. He really was a sweet guy. "So what are you thinking of going to school for?" I asked him trying to focus on anything else.

He smiled at me, his big boyish grin that forced a giggle from my lips. He truly had become a beautiful man. "I want to go for photography."

26

This made me laugh, "Oh?"

"Yeah," He was excited now which I appreciated, "you want to see my portfolio."

I put my pen and paper down on the couch and looked at him, "I really do." I said and he jumped up and ran to his room.

"I think you may have just made his whole year." Allie said walking into the room smiling. "He's wanted to show you for months."

I smiled, "it's nice to have something else to think about."

She nodded at me, "then I shall save my line of questioning until you're ready to focus again."

I laughed, "oh Allie always my practical side." I said. "Besides I haven't really decided what I am going to do."

"No one expects you to. It's only been two days." She smiled at me. "But I know how your mind works Emma; I know it's something that you're going to be thinking about."

"I'm going back to school."

"Are you sure, I am sure they would be ok if you took the rest of the semester off."

"It's only a few more months. I can make it through, and then I have the whole summer to figure out what I am going to do with... well to figure out what I want to do."

"That's my girl," she said. Just then Brandon walked back into the room with his portfolio, a huge grin on his face. "Look at him; he's like a little kid."

He rolled his eyes at her and then came to wedge himself on the couch between us. "Move over." He said to Allie smiling. She moved over slightly and laughed. He put the portfolio on my lap and put his arm around me so he could look over my shoulder as I looked. Allie laughed at him and got up to come sit on my other side. "Where you going?" he asked her

"I want to see too. Do I not get to look?"

He rolled his eyes at her, "yeah fine." He smiled at me and showed me his photos. They were actually good, better than good they were fantastic. When I got to the last page he tried to take the portfolio back before I could look at the photo. It was a picture of me sitting on a swing in his back yard from the summer. I was laughing and looking at, I assume, Allie. I looked happy and carefree; I looked... beautiful and very unlike myself. I had no idea he was taking the picture.

"Wow!" I said and looked at him

"Yeah, sorry I guess I should have asked you before I put a picture of you in there huh?" he blushed.

"That's a great picture," Allie said to him. "I mean really great, she looks beautiful." I gave her a dirty look, "oh, you know what I mean," she said and I laughed.

"Elmer's glue people look good in black and white, it's our color scheme." I said smiling at him. "I'm impressed Brandon, these are all so good. You're going to be an amazing photographer. And this picture..." I said looking down at it again, "well I don't think I have ever looked this good, so thank you."

He shook his head at me and rolled his eyes at his sister. "What do you see when you look in the mirror?" He whispered. I was pretty sure he didn't mean for me to hear it. "Thanks Emma," he said. "It means a lot that you think so." I smiled at him. "So, is there anything on that list of yours we can help with?"

"I don't think so. I don't think I am ready to do half of it and the other half I have already done."

Allie nodded and put her arm around me. "We are here when you're ready." She said. She picked up my list and looked it over. "Yeah I will definitely help you with this stuff, none of it is pleasant."

CHAPTER FIVE

The next few days went by in a fog. I made it through both wakes and the funeral, the brunch after the funeral and the hundreds of the "I'm so sorry's" with Allie holding me up on one side and Brandon on the other.

The only time I had to spend alone was when I gave the eulogy. I stood up in front of all of these people and watched as they cried. I talked about how my father would play golf every Sunday in the summer even though he never got any better, "Emma," he would say, "it's just a hobby, and if it makes me happy when I'm doing it, who cares if I'm any good at it." Then he would grin at me and say, "remember that when you finally find something your terrible at'. Like most fathers, mine was convinced I was the best at everything." I smiled at the memory and choked back the tears. "He was a great man, he was great at his job, and he loved his family with a passion few men will ever posses in their lifetime"

"My mother was kind and gentle. A graphic designer by trade, but I remember having to sit for hours as a little kid while she painted me. 'Just a little longer pumpkin I promise then you can paint me.' she would smile and kiss my forehead. When I decided to become a photographer she was elated I had followed in her footsteps. 'I'm so happy, investment banking is dreadfully boring' she would say then giggle when my father would try to protest. When I was accepted to school she took me on a tour of New England for a week and all we did was take pictures." I stopped for a moment and looked out at the crowd. About all I could see was Brandon sitting in the front row towering over everyone. I smiled at him and he winked back. "My parents," I started again, "where the most amazing people I know and I will miss them more than these words will ever justify. Thank you all for coming." I walked back to my seat and Allie and Brandon wrapped their arms around me. I had made it through this part, only a few more hours of rooms full of strangers.

At the brunch I talked a grown man out of a suicidal rant about how much he loved my father and what a great man he was and how he would be miss. I always found it amusing how the family seems to always console the visitors in situations like this. Shouldn't they be consoling me? But I was almost glad they weren't, because how would I handle that.

A few days after the funeral, I got phone calls from both my mother and father's companies. I had to go in and meet with their life insurance plan managers and I was assured, despite my best efforts that such a matter could not possibly wait until I had finished grieving. So I went to each and my dynamic duo came with me. I got looks from them as if to say, shouldn't you have brought an adult. One man actually had the nerve to ask at my father's company.

"Shouldn't you be here with a guardian?" he asked almost annoyed.

I glared at him, "well, you insisted that despite the fact I have lost both my parents in the last week, therefore negating any existence of a biological family I may have, I had to come and settle the matter of my father's life insurance policy and also that on my last birthday I turned eighteen therefore officially making me an adult I don't feel that even if neither of these things were true that you would have any right to ask me about the where abouts of my guardian. If it had been such a concern for you, or if you had looked at the policy itself which clearly states my birthday, you could have asked or simply known without my need to tell you that I do not, in fact, need a guardian." I sat back in the chair and glared at him and everyone in the room stared at me.

The man chuckled slightly. "You have to be Roger's kid; you sounded just like him just then." I smiled at the man and we finished our business. By the time I was done talking to all of the lawyers and plan admins for life insurance and 401K plans I was exhausted. I wanted a little bit of time where I didn't have to be an adult. When the last thing was signed and I was waiting for the papers from the probate court to come back to take care of their bank accounts I decided I wanted to go home.

"We'll come with you." Allie said looking at Brandon.

"No, I really just want to be alone right now. If you don't hear from me in two days you can come check on me." I said and smiled.

When I walked into the house alone for the first time, it felt empty in a way I can't describe. I climbed up the stairs to my parent's bedroom and laid across the bed sobbing into a pillow, and that is where I stayed for 2 days getting up only to use the bathroom.

My parents had been amazing people. They were both funny and smart. My Dad was an investment banker in Boston. He had a pretty stuffy job, but he was anything but. He use to take me to Sox games all the time and we would sing and heckle the other team. He played the guitar, not well of course, but he played it. My mom told me that is how they had met.

"I was walking through the campus on my way to class and this pretension jerk was sitting under a tree playing a guitar with a gaggle of girls around him." My mother would say and then they would share a smile as if there was more to the story that they didn't want to tell me.

"Stop exaggerating Naomi." He would say with a chuckle, "it wasn't a gaggle." He would say to me, "it was only about five."

"That's a gaggle." My mother and I would both say with a giggle.

The story was always the same and they told it every year on their anniversary, but I never got tired of it. "He jumped up from the ground when I walked by and yelled for me to stop."

"She's a fast walker." He would say with another chuckled.

"Well you were trying to out run a gaggle of screaming girls." I would joke.

My mom would laugh and put her arm around me as they finished the story. My mother ignored him all the way to class, and again when he waited for her outside and then followed her back to her dorm. "I should have called the campus security." She smiled.

"I was harmless."

"I didn't know that then." He would just look at her and she would laugh, "Ok I did, but it would have taught you a lesson. I had no interest in him." She would say looking at me.

"But I wore you down." He smiled triumphantly.

She would laugh quietly, "yes you did dear, and then, as soon as I gave in I fell madly in love with him."

"And then we had you kido." My dad would beam at me. "Our little miracle."

"I thought you would never come." My mom would say and squeeze me then kiss my head. My parents had tried for five years before my mother got pregnant with me. That's why I am an only child. She just couldn't get pregnant,

I looked like my mother. We were both short and curvy, my hair was long strawberry blonde like hers and my eyes were a pale blue. When I smiled they would almost disappear. She was a little shorter than me; about five two and her laugh could make you smile even without seeing her face. She taught me that life should never be taken so seriously that you lose sight of what makes you blissful.

My dad was handsome; he was about six feet tall with brown hair and brown eyes. He was funny to the point where my Mom and I would spit a drink across the room at least once a week. He was the kind of Dad that made Daddies girls a reasonable thing. He taught me how to build things, balance my check book and change my own oil in my car. They were the kind of parents that I knew, when I told people about them, they thought I was making them up. But they had wanted to be parents so badly that when they finally were, they never took a second of it for granted.

I thought about this as I lay across their bed and stared at a picture of the three of us on their nightstand. For two days I couldn't even bear to move. I couldn't eat and I barely slept. I just finally gave myself the time I needed to grieve without having to worry about anything or anyone else.

When I had been alone for two days there was a knock at bedroom door. When I picked up my head I realized that I felt better, not great and not even close to normal, but better and that's a step in the right direction.

"Come in" I said.

Brandon poked his head around the door. "Hi beautiful, it's been two days I just came to check on you." he smiled.

I smiled back at him, "you can come in." I said. "Beautiful." I repeated and laughed. I looked anything but beautiful. My eyes were puffy and red and my hair was in knots on my head. He walked in the room as I got up and went to the dresser for a brush.

"How are you doing?" he asked, his face loaded with concern.

"Better." I said and smiled. "Not great, but better. I didn't really give myself time to grieve before." I popped a mint into my mouth.

"You were a busy girl." He said and smiled as I went and sat down next to him on the bed.

"Where's your sister?" I asked

"She went to get Chinese food. She wanted me to check on you and see if you wanted some. She told me to tell you she got egg rolls and scallion pancakes."

I laughed, "She's a good friend." I said. "And so are you." I told him and put my hand on his shoulder. "I don't know how I would have made it through the last week without you. You and your sister are the best friends anyone could have. Thank you." I kissed him on the cheek and he immediately began to blush. I wanted to kiss him again, to run my hands through his hair and kiss those beautiful lips.

I think he may have caught my mood because he smiled and blushed a little more. "As much as I would love for you to do what I think you are thinking right now, and if you think it will make you feel better I will certainly take the hit for the team," he grinned at me and I giggled, "I am still only fifteen years old, you're still three years older than me, and you are still going to be leaving to go back to school. If after all that, you still want to kiss me? Then please do."

I smiled at him and laughed. "I still want to kiss you, but it wouldn't be right to kiss you." I got up from the bed and kissed him on the forehead.

"You want to kiss me?"

"Of course I want to kiss you."

"That's crazy, you're crazy." He said shaking his head. "Why would you possibly want to kiss me?"

"What do *you* see when you look in the mirror?" I said and smiled as I walked out of the room.

He came out of the room after me. "If I have to spend the rest of my life as your best friend slash little brother type I am not missing what could be my only opportunity where you actually want me to kiss you." he pulled me into his arms and paused for a moment as he looked in my eyes. I smiled at him and he leaned in and kissed me. I felt like I had electricity shooting from my toes to the top of my head. I wrapped my arms around him tighter, even if it hadn't been the most amazing kiss of my life; it was still nice to feel something other than sad. Our lips moved together in perfect rhythm, he smelt like a combination of shaving cream and old spice.

When I could feel myself starting the wrap around him I pulled away. I grinned at him. "Holy Crap." He said and laughed. I let go of his neck and got back onto the floor. "You were holding back last summer." He said smiling.

"Wow! So were you." he grinned smugly. "We should go." I said. He frowned slightly and I laughed. "Your sister will come here if we are gone too long." He nodded. "And I can't be… well I can't be responsible for my actions. You mean too much to me to do something stupid."

"No more kissing then?"

I laughed, "No more kissing." I said. But even as I said it I didn't know if I could stick to it. I knew that I couldn't date Brandon, not now, he was too young and…well I just couldn't. I would have to forget about the way I felt when he was around me. It was just a little crush and I would get over it someday, wouldn't I?

CHAPTER SIX

The last week of vacation I finished up some last minutes things. I decided to deal with the accounts, the house and everything else when I came home for the summer. There was no reason to rush things. I wasn't ready to let go of them yet. On the last day before Allie and I went back to school, she and Brandon asked if I would take a ride with them.

"Where are we going?" I asked

"Just somewhere I think you will like," Brandon answered

I looked at Allie and she just shook her head, "this is all him, I'm just the driver."

I turned back and looked at him. "You are the most impatient woman I have ever met Emma Grace, just wait." I pouted a little but I knew he would take me to some place to try and cheer me up.

"Ok you have to close your eyes," he said to me when we got on the highway,

"What?" I exclaimed turning in my seat to look back at him again.

"Please Emma, just close them." He said.

I did as I was told and the three of us drove for a little longer. I could feel Allie pulling off the highway and parking. "Can I open my eyes now?" I asked.

"Nope not yet," Brandon said. "I promise I'll make sure you don't fall down while we are walking.

I laughed, "Or you could just let me see where I am going." I tried again.

Allie laughed, "Knock it off Peters, and just keep your eyes shut." I made a grunting noise but kept my eyes closed.

Brandon came around and helped me out of the car, taking my arm and leading me down the street. He picked me up briefly to run me across the street. When we finally stopped he positioned me to face something. "Ok open em," He said

I opened my eyes to see that I was standing on Yawkey way facing Fenway Park. "Oh Brandon," I said as the tears started to fall.

"You told me this was your happy place so I thought I would take you here and maybe it would cheer you up, even just a little bit."

Allie was staring at her brother in awe as was I. "What have you done with my brother?" she said with a laugh. He grinned back at her and I lunged at him, wrapping my arms around him.

"Thank you, thank you so much." I said.

He leaned down and kissed the top of my head. "We're going in" he said.

"We are?" Allie and I both asked.

"Yeah, Dad's friend works in security here and when I told him what I wanted to do for you, he made a call. He's going to meet us inside."

"You're amazing," I said.

He just smiled down at me and took my hand walking towards gate A. Steve's friend met us when we were inside and let the rest of the guys know why we were there. I walked into the grandstand seats down towards the dugout. I ran my hand over the top of it and smiled. I walked all around, touching Peski's pole, and Yaz's. I put my hand on the green monster. Everything about the place made me smile. Everything about it made me think of my Dad and the amazing times we had here. The last place I went was to his seats. The seats I had spent so many days and nights in with him and my mom. She was as obsessed with them as my father and I were and it was one of our favorite family events. We watched every game and just crossed out fingers like every other fan that this was our year. The seats belonged to a guy my father worked with. He traveled a lot so my dad went halves in the tickets with him because he would take all the games the man couldn't make it to. The seats were right behind home plate about fifteen rows up. They were amazing, but it was easy to get them when you were on an almost eighty year world series drought, but none of that matter to us, they were our team and it was something and some place that would always keep me connected to them. I stood staring at the seats for what felt like ages. I felt Allie's hand on my shoulder for comfort and I sat down. They both sat in the row behind me. We sat there in complete silence for a long time. I just stared out over the field.

"I want to be proposed to here," I finally said. I heard Allie and Brandon laugh behind me. I turned and looked at both of them. "I'm serious."

"We know," Allie said with a smile, "that's why we are laughing." They both grinned at me and I laughed.

I turned back around and looked out over the field again. "Even empty this place is electric." I watched the grounds crew work as they started getting ready for the upcoming season and I realized for sure that this was not going to kill me and my parents would want me to be happy. I smiled and got up, "ok, I'm ready to go now." I kissed Brandon on the cheek before he could get up. "You are amazing, thank you for this; you have no idea what this does for my soul."

"I'm glad," he said and kissed my forehead as he stood up.

I kept in touch with both of them for the rest of the semester. Allie called me every night. Brandon would send me e-mails about whatever girl he was dating at the time. I would always get a pang of jealousy when I read then, which I am not entirely sure was not his intention to begin with. But I was happy for him. I left my love life out of the e-mails to Brandon, although his sister knew every detail. I spent every holiday and summer at their house.

CHAPTER SEVEN

After Allie and I graduated from school she moved back to MA and I got a job at a photography studio on Quincy called "MacKay Studios" I sold my parents house and I bought my own house the next year and they both helped me fix it up. One day after Brandon had gone back to school again, Allie was in my kitchen with me drinking coffee.

"So are you ever going to tell me what happened with you and my brother? The two of you look like you are pain when you are near each other and you're not somehow touching." She looked at me quizzically.

"I don't know what you're talking about." I said looking down at my cup of coffee. It was the day after Brandon had left to go back to school. I was 23 now, he was 20. The good bye had been awkward. He held me close for a long time and he kept kissing head, but he never kissed more than my head after that night five years before. Even though I made attempts to let him know I wanted him too. But part of me was glad he didn't because I still wasn't sure about it. Little did I know, this would be our last good bye like this for a long time.

"You know exactly what I am talking about, our last girls' night before school. Ever since then things have been a little weird between the two of you and I want to know why." I just shrugged at her and smirked over my coffee cup. She threw a muffin at me. "You infuriate me" she said.

I shrugged again. "He kissed me." I said plainly.

"I KNEW IT!!" she exclaimed causing me to jump then laugh. "I can't believe you never told me this"

"It was a long time ago Allie. I don't think he even remembers, or cares. And I think you may be crazy."

She glared at me. "You're such an idiot" she said

"Excuse me?"

"'I don't even think he remembers'" she shook her head as she imitated me. "You're and idiot. That boy has had a crush on you forever. I highly doubt that he doesn't remember."

I rolled my eyes at her. "It doesn't matter. Like I said it was a long time ago and besides he is still too young for me."

She raised one eyebrow at me. "Is that your only excuse?" she asked smiling.

I thought for a minute. "Um... I don't know anymore."

"Hmm" she said. "Well he will never be less than three years younger than you." I nodded. "We'll see what happens." She said smirking at me.

"You sound like you want me to date your brother." I said

"Yup you're an idiot," she said laughing and the conversation about Brandon was over.

The next year the Red Sox won the World Series for the first time in eighty six years. Allie actually watched it with me as we sat on the phone with Brandon. I never doubted, even for a second that this was our year. 3-0 to the Yankee's seemed like nothing, we would overcome it. When Damon hit the grand slam in game 7 I knew it was over. And I cried when Folk threw Edgar Rentaria out at first to sweep the Cardinals and win the series. I bought every flag and banner I could and put them on my parent's graves. Allie came with me and the two of us almost giggled as we decorated the head stone.

"We did it," I said. Because like any true fan I refer to the team like I am actually part of it. "I hope they get sox games up there." I said and smiled. Brandon was on the phone most of the time we were at the graveyard.

When Brandon graduated a couple of years later, he never came home. He decided that he was going to go backpacking before he settled into a permanent job. He had gone to school for photography like he had said and wanted to take pictures of the world.

I think that is when I decided holding a candle for a few kisses I had when I was eighteen was ridiculous, no matter how amazing they were. It was at that moment I decided to move on completely.

CHAPTER EIGHT

Shortly after my twenty-eight birthday I re-met my boss's son Michael Mackay. He had recently graduated from law school and had gotten a job at one of the most prestigious law firms in Boston. He owned a condo near Park Street and he was one of the most beautiful creatures I have ever laid eyes on, and for some unknown reason he seemed to be interested in me. He was about 6'2; he had sandy blonde hair and eyes so crystal clear blue you could swim in them. I met him at a dinner at his parents' house. Bob and Sophie MacKay had pretty much adopted me when I started working for them. Bob was my boss; he was a tall balding man who loved photography as much as I did. He made the work day go quickly to the point where you were almost sad it was over. He was also as big a sox fan as me. He reminded me of my Dad and I loved working for him.

They had been having me over for dinner ever Thursday night for about four years, starting about a year after I was hired.

"You are like the daughter we never had." Sophie would say almost every week. She was beautiful. She has about five ten with blonde hair and sparkling blue eyes.

I would smile and thank her. Bob and Sophie had been amazing, so when Michael came home from law school and started having dinner with us I was excited. He was charming and funny and he seemed to like spending time with his parents as much as I did. I liked being around him, but I never thought I stood a chance to be anything more than his friend.

The first time he asked me to dinner, I looked around the room to make sure he was talking to me. Which made him laugh; he had a very sexy laugh. He took me to dinner and we closed the restaurant we were talking for so long. He took me home and walked me to my door. My stomach was doing somersaults and he just smiled at me.

"I had a really great time with you tonight Emma. You're kind of, well... You're kind of amazing."

I blushed and smiled at him. "I had a great time too." I said

He smiled again. "Would you mind terribly if I kissed you? I have sort of been thinking about it all night." I looked at him quizzically, he just smiled and leaned over pushing a stray piece of hair from my face, and then he kissed me. It was soft and gentle, it was nice. It wasn't the best kiss of my life, but it was definitely second. It made me a little light headed when he pulled away. He had a goofy grin on his face, which made me giggle. "Wow!" he said. "That was better than I imagined it would be."

I looked at him feigning hurt. "You didn't think it would be good?" I asked smiling.

He laughed again. "No I knew it would be good, I just didn't think it would be that good." I smiled and realized that I could really fall for this guy.

On our second date Michael took me to a Red Sox game. Bob had season tickets and he let us use them for the day. I could tell from the very beginning that Michael had only suggested it because he knew I was such a big fan, but he was a good sport and we had a lot of fun.

After the game we went and had a couple of beers at Cask 'N' Flaggon, a bar right outside Fenway Park. The extra beer was probably not the best idea since we had already had a little too much during the game to begin with. I was having fun, more fun than I had remembered having in a long time. Michael was incredibly charming and funny. He held my hand most of the day and it felt as if I was the only girl in the room when he looked at me.

"Did you have fun today?" he asked me.

"I did," I said with a grin. "I can't remember the last time I had this much fun."

He chuckled and kissed my hand. "Good, I am very glad."

I giggled, I really couldn't help myself. I was more than a little drunk at this point and he was terribly handsome. Plus he was looking at me with those gorgeous blue eyes, he almost took my breath away. "You're beautiful." I said and then immediately wanted to slap myself.

He chuckled again, "not nearly as beautiful as you," he said and kissed me.

I smiled at him again, "we should eat," I said suddenly remembering we hadn't eaten anything but a hot dog at the beginning of the game.

"You want to order something?' he asked looking around for the waitress.

"No, why don't we go back to your house and I will make us something to eat," I grinned.

He turned and looked at me with one eyebrow raised. When he saw the grin on my face he smirked. I raised my eyebrows in a vaudeville villain esk way and he took out his wallet and threw money on the table. "Let's go," he said taking me hand.

"Aren't you even going to wait for the bill?" I asked with a giggle.

He turned back around and smiled, "that's more than covers it. I have much more pressing matters to deal with." And then he kissed me before whisking me out of the bar.

When we got back to his apartment I didn't get the chance to make him dinner. As soon as we were in the elevator he started kissing me. He fumbled with his keys when we got to his door. "You in a hurry for something?" I asked with a giggle.

He just smirked at me again and flung the door open, "ladies first," Was all he said.

I walked into his apartment, it was beautiful. There was a huge window on the far side of the room that overlooked the park. The furniture was very bachelor pad. The look of the place made me smile. It was definitely something his parents had helped him buy. There was no way he could afford a place like this on his salary, being right out of law school. I didn't have much time to look around because once the door was closed behind him he spun me around and kissed me again. "You know," I started when he moved to kissing my neck. "I don't normally go back to men's apartments on the second date."

"Good," he said with a chuckle. "That makes me special." I giggled and he took my hand and walked me towards the bedroom. "And besides, if you count all of the dinners we have had with my parents over the last few months, I would say this is at least our eighth date."

"I like the way you think Mr. Mackay," I said and kissed him. We fell back onto the bed and the conversation was over. It was amazing; it was definitely something that needed a repeat performance. Michael was an unexpectedly unselfish lover. When we were lying in his bed after and I propped myself up on my hand and looked at him. "Wow!" I said with a smile

He chuckled and even blushed a little, something that caught me off guard. I had only known him for a few months at this point but I knew one thing for certain, Michael was a very confident man, sometimes overly so. So when he seemed a little embarrassed by my compliment I was delighted. "Wow yourself. That was amazing. I mean… amazing." He grinned up at me and rested his arms behind his head.

It was the first time I had looked at him when he wasn't fully clothed. He was even more beautiful like this. I could barely take my eyes off of him. His skin was still a little tan from a trip to Mexico he had taken a few weeks before. I traced my finger along his bicep. He was perfect, which suddenly made me very self conscience about my fluffiness. As if reading my mind he pulled me into his arms and kissed my forehead. "You are beautiful," he said, "absolutely beautiful."

I squeezed him and kissed his chest, "thank you." I smiled at him. "You want me to make you dinner now?"

He thought about it for a minute then nodded, "I would love for you to make me dinner."

I jumped out of the bed and he watched me walk over to the door. I leaned down to pick up my clothes to start to put them back on and he frowned. I laughed, "Do you think I am going to cook you dinner in the nude?"

"I man can dream can't he? I was actually hoping you would cook it in like an apron and some pearls." He chuckled and leaned back on his arms again.

I rolled my eyes at him, "typical man," I said with a laugh and pulled my jeans and shirt on. "So what do you have to eat in this place?" I called to him while I was walking towards the kitchen.

"Not sure," he called back. "I think I might have some chicken." He said as he came up behind me kissing my neck. He had put on a pair of pajama pants and I smiled at him. "Hey if you put clothes on I am going to put some on too."

"Oh, it's only fair." I said with a laugh and kissed him. I made us dinner and we sat and talked some more. It was hands down the best second date I had ever had.

Michael was amazing. He was funny and smart, and even though I knew he thought what I did for a living was silly and a bit childish, he never made me feel that way for a very long time. For the first year and a half Michael worked as an assistant on big cases and did some small ones of his own. He would basically gofer for the lead lawyers. He worked a lot, but I saw him most nights. Ally liked him. She thought he was a little stuffy, but otherwise he was a decent guy.

"He clearly adores you, I like that." She said one day with a smile. We were having a cookout in my back yard about nine months after Michael and I started dating.

"He does, doesn't he," I said with a giggle. He turned around and winked at me. Brandon was even supportive from wherever he was at the time. We would e-mail each other almost every day. I didn't get to talk to him on the phone much, but I took what I could get. Everything was perfect. I loved my job; I loved my boyfriend and with the exception of not having Brandon in the country my life was perfect.

CHAPTER NINE

About a year and a half into our relationship
Michael started taking on bigger cases. He started
canceling dates all the time and I saw less and less
of him. I tried to convince myself that I was just
over reacting. It seemed to work for a while because
he was still the same sweet and kind man that I had
fallen so completely in love it. I could handle seeing
him less; after all I did have my own life. It's what
came a few months after that started to become hard
to take.

We were at dinner at my favorite restaurant. He
had been about twenty minutes late, but I didn't
give him a hard time. I got it; this was the life of a
lawyer's girlfriend. So I smiled and kissed him
when he came in. "Hi Babe," I said to him when he
was sitting down.

He smiled at me half heartedly, "Hi Beautiful, how
was your day?"

"It was long, I'm exhausted," I said but smiled. As
true as it was I wouldn't have it any other way. He
made a scoffing noise and I narrowed my eyes at
him. "How was your day Michael?"

His eyes widened at my tone and he saw the look of
annoyance on my face. His own faced softened and

he chuckled. "It was not a good day my love, but I am sorry I laughed when you said you had a long day that was uncalled for."

I smiled back at him and shrugged, "no problem," I said and winked at him. He laughed again. "Anything I can do to help?" I asked moving my hand so the waitress could put my drink down. We ordered our dinners and she left.

"You can give me a back rub when we get back to your house, that would help a lot," He said with a wink.

I giggled and shook my head at him. He told me a little more about his day and the waitress brought us our food. When I started telling him about the project I was working on I could tell I was starting to lose him. "We had a shoot in the park this morning. I haven't been in Foreriver field since I was in Junior High school it was kind of surreal, but fun, you know?"

"Hmm," he answered.

I looked up at him and he seemed to be paying a little bit of attention. This was a common thing lately. I would start to talk about work and his eyes would glaze over. It annoyed me because I would listen to him drone on and on for hours about files and depositions and he couldn't seem to give me twenty minutes to tell him about my work. "Your dad and I worked hard on getting this client. They are starting a sports club for kids and they want us to do all the fliers and catalogs." I smiled but then quickly frowned when I realized he had gone into full glazed mode. "And then this crazy alien ship came down and landed right in the middle of the field. It was amazing."

"Hmm," he said again.

I was growing more impatient with each passing moment. "So I got to spend the day driving around the galaxy." He just smiled a little and nodded. "MICHAEL," I said as loud as I could without drawing too much attention to us.

He seemed to snap back to life, "huh? What? What happened?" he looked at me and the face I was making must have reflected my anger. "What Emma?" he said with his own annoyance.

"You know you could at least listen to me when I tell you about my day," I could feel the tears stinging my eyes, but there was no way I was going to start crying.

"I was listening," he said even more annoyed than he had been just a second ago.

"Oh really, Then what was I talking about?" I crossed my arms across my chest.

"You were talking about your day and you did a photo shoot at a park."

"What park?"

"Emma please, don't be a pain."

"Oh so I am a pain for asking you to pay attention to me for ten minutes while I tell you about my day. I am so terribly sorry Michael, I remember to keep it short from now on."

His face hardened and he put his hands on the table, "oh and I suppose you listen to me all the time?"

"I do."

"Then what case am I working on right now then?"

"You are working on a hit and run case. You are currently waiting for some labs to come back to see if the blood that was found on the dashboard of the accused car matches your victim. You have a pretty good feeling that it will and you will have an open and shut case."

He looked at me and his jaw dropped, "Emma… I…"

"What Michael? Didn't know I actually listen when you speak to me. Yes I do that is what you do when the person you love is telling you about their day.

You listen to what they have to say, good or bad even if you have no interest in the subject at hand."

"I am so sorry Emm, really truly I am." He looked sorry.

"This happens a lot lately Michael; you glaze over when I start talking about work. It makes me sad. I understand that you don't think what I do is really a job, but it is. I work hard and I am good at it, and I love it. I love you and I want you to at least try to be more supportive, like you used to be."

He smiled warmly at me. Those big blue eyes sparkling and it was like I was turned to mush. He reached over and took one of the flowers out of the vase on the table "for you my love."

He gave me a carnation and I made a face of disgust at it. I hated carnations. I laughed, "thank you," I said. "These things remind me of being in high school. I mean they don't even smell good, most ridiculous flower ever."

He chuckled and shook his head. "I think they are kind of pretty."

"Yuck," I said again.

He chuckled again and paid the bill. I re-told him the story in the way home, this time leaving out the alien parts and he actually seemed to listen to

everything. I understood that he was never going to
be completely behind what I did for a living, even
though his father was my boss and he had reaped
the benefits of what my profession could do. I
understood that sometimes people just see art as a
hobby and not a good way of making a living. For a
while I thought that was ok, that I could handle
someone not entirely respecting what I did for a
living. Like I said it wasn't for everyone.

CHAPTER TEN

The turning point for Allie came on my twenty
ninth birthday. I had made dinner and had a few
friends over to celebrate. Michael was more than
two hours late. We waited for him for about an
hour when I decided we were going to eat without
him. I went into the kitchen to pull the food out of
the warm oven and Allie followed me.

"Has he called?" she asked. She could no longer
hide her annoyance that he was always late and
often forgot about things all together.

I picked my phone up off the counter and looked at
it, "nope," I said and pulled the chicken from the
oven.

She knew it would only make me feel worse if she
showed me how angry she was, even though I could
tell without her saying anything. She just put her
hand on back and said, "He'll be here."

"I know," I said with a half smile. "He's always
late." I couldn't decide what was upsetting me
more, the fact that he was over an hour late for my
birthday party, or the fact that he hadn't called yet.

I brought the food out and we all ate and drank wine
and talked. Brandon called halfway through dinner

to sing to me. He sang terribly, but I was glad he called since it was far too rare for me to hear his voice. About two and a half hours after the party had started, Michael walked through the door holding a bouquet of carnations.

"I am so sorry I am late everyone," he said waving at everyone as he came over to kiss me. "I'm so sorry," he whispered in my ear. I could smell the alcohol on his breath.

"Have you been drinking?" I asked him narrowing my eyes.

"I had a beer after work, I won my case," he beamed at me.

"Congratulations, I am very happy that you won your case babe, but you are two and a half hour late. I would have taken you out to celebrate tomorrow. And besides I'm not stupid, you don't smell like beer you smell like whiskey."

He rolled his eyes at me, "calm down," he said. He pulled a chair up next to me and turned to talk to my friend Jack.

I thought for a split second that maybe I was over reacting. I mean he should be able to celebrate after winning a big case. Then I caught a glimpse of the clock. It was almost nine thirty and court had gotten out around three. Allie squeezed my hand, "deep breaths Emm, deep breaths."

I took her advice and took a few. It would have calmed me if I wasn't breathing in the smell of whiskey coming off of Michael. I clenched my fists and thought to myself that I wasn't going to let this ruin my night.

Suddenly Michael stood up. "I want to make a toast," he said smiling down at me. Everyone looked at each other and shrugged grabbing their glasses. It was more obvious than it had been when he came in that he had, had more than a couple of drinks, that he was completely drunk. "To my Emma," he started leaning down to kiss the top of my head. "Whose foolish optimism and charming career path she has chosen make her the most adorable woman on the planet." As his speech went on more and more glasses were put back onto the table until all ten people were just staring up at him, mouths gaping. He finished the speech of continued backward compliments with, "to Emma's last birthday in her twenties and her hopeful spring into adulthood." He put his glass in the air and then drank it down in a single sip; no one joined him they just looked around the table uncomfortably.

Allie however was not as quiet, "what the hell is wrong with you?" she said standing up. She looked down at my face, which must have looked like I was as close to tears as I was because she stopped herself from spewing all the things she had to say. Instead she picked up her glass and said, "To MY Emma, the kindest, sweetest hardest working person I have ever known. You are like my sister and you deserve all the good that this world has to offer. To Emma's last birthday in her twenties and a spring into pure happiness, I love you Emma Grace." She lifted her glass in the air, "to Emma," everyone said and drank. She leaned down to kiss the top of my head and a smiled up at her. Michael chuckled beside me. I looked at him and I could actually feel my heart breaking.

The party dispersed and Allie helped me clean up while Michael fought with someone on his phone. When the kitchen was done Allie wrapped her arms around me, "I can stay if you want," she said.

I smiled at her and shook my head. "No I'll be fine. I think Michael and I have a few things to discuss."

She smiled back at me and nodded, "ok then. Happy birthday Emma, I love you to pieces."

"I love you too," I said and hugged her good bye.

I sat on a chair in my living room and looked through some of the cards that people had given me for my birthday. Michael paced around to room talking. About fifteen minutes after Allie left my phone rang. I looked at it and it was Brandon. I laughed because I knew the only reason he was calling was because Allie had told him about the speech that Michael had made tonight. I picked up, "hello?" I said.

"Hello beautiful," he said back to me.

"Twice in one day, now don't I feel like the luckiest girl in the world," I said with a giggle. My laugh must have caught Michael's attention because he turned to look at me.

"I am calling to see how the party went."

"I bet you are," I said laughing again.

"What does that mean," he said with a chuckled trying to fake surprise.

"So your sister told you then,"

"She may have mentioned something. Are you ok?"

"Yeah I'm fine Hun," the Hun caught his attention again and Michael hung up the phone and came across the room and sat on the couch facing me.

"You know I am here if you need me," he said.

"In a manner of speaking."

He laughed, "Well I am always available to listen anyway, even if I am not physically there."

I laughed again, "Yes I know that. But hey, can I email you later, I think there is another conversation I have to have at the moment."

"Is he staring at you?"

"Yup."

"Does he look mad or sad?"

"A little of both and confused."

Brandon chuckled on the other end, "ok I will let you go then, I love ya face Emma Grace." His rhyme made me giggle.

"Love you a ton Brandon," I said trying to make my own rhyme.

"Close," he said laughing. "Happy birthday I will talk to you soon."

"Thanks B, night."

I hung up the phone and turned back to look at Michael. He was still sitting on the couch and he looked like he was in pain. "Good," I thought to myself. "Well," I started, "I sure hope you have a good explanation for that display." He just stared at me and shook his head. "You ruined my birthday

Michael, well you almost ruined it, and you weren't here long enough to actually ruin it." He opened his mouth to say something but stopped himself. It was the first time since we had been dating that he did not have an answer for what I had to say. "Why would you say those things, is that what you really think?" he didn't say anything, "Talk Michael!"

"I'm sorry," he said. "I am so sorry I can't even find the right words to convey to you just how sorry I am Emma."

"Is that what you really think? I realize you think that my job is silly, you think I should be a photo journalist or something if I am going to take pictures for a living, and I realize that I am overly optimistic about life, but buddy it has saved your butt more than once in this relationship."

"I know," he said.

"And as for me being an adult, I have been an adult since I was eighteen years old. I had to deal with things in my life that I am glad you have never had to deal with. You don't even know what being an adult is like Michael, your parents have done everything for you, your whole life, and I didn't get the luxury. Yes I have things because of my parent's death, but I would trade anything in the world to change that. So don't you dare say that this is the year I 'spring into adulthood' because sweetheart that year was 1998."

He stared at me for a minute, "I'm… I'm going to explain myself, but it will in no way make up for what I did. I just want you to know where in my messed up head all of that came from." He reached out and took my hand. "I have no excuse for being so late, none. But when I came in and you were so angry even after I told you I won my case, it just made me mad, furious really, like you didn't care…"

"Michael I…"

"Let me finish Emm. I know that you care; I know why you are angry. I am just explaining where my logic was coming from, what little I had anyway. I was furious that you cared more about some dinner party than me, so I wanted to make you feel as bad as I did."

I just stared at him for a minute, he was right it didn't make me feel better. "Are you twelve?" I asked him fuming again.

"More like eight I think," he said sadly.

"You do know that the main reason I was so angry that you were late is not because you were out celebrating but because you never bothered to call me to either let me know you were going to be late, or to even let me know you had won your case to begin with."

"I do."

"And some dinner party? Michael it's my fucking birthday, my birthday. I get that some people don't make a big deal, but you know I do."

"I know."

"It's the one day of the year I want you to make ME the center of attention. For god sakes I spend countless nights with your lawyer friends and their wives who think I am some freak, but I never complain because it makes you happy." I stared down at him and tears started to form at the corners of his eyes. "You never come to dinner at your parents with me anymore; you can't be bothered to spend time with them."

"The only reason I went to those dinners in the first place was to be around you," he said looking up at me.

I thought it was sweet and I almost caved when he said it, but I didn't. "You broke my heart tonight Michael."

"I don't believe a word I said," he finally said.

"What?"

"Not a single word I said except for you being adorable."

"Don't try to be all cute so I forgive you."

"I'm not I swear," he answered. He looked like he was telling the truth so I let him continue. "I think you are amazing and your funny and I love that you always look on the bright side because it is something I am incapable of. I do hate what you do for a living, but because I think you are better than it. You are the most loving and nurturing woman I know and there is no way you could be that if you also weren't the most adult woman I know. I love you Emma, it is the one thing I am the most sure of in the world. Please, please forgive me."

I looked down at his clearly heartbroken face and wanted to kiss him. I wanted to forgive him right there and go upstairs and salvage what was left of the last few hours of my birthday. But I didn't, he didn't deserve it right then. "I had a wonderful birthday despite your display." He looked down again. "You can sleep on the couch tonight, or you can go home," I said walking towards the stairs to my bedroom. "But I highly suggest you sleep right where you are if you even want to think about continuing this conversation in the morning."

"I'll stay here, I'll be right here when you wake up."

"Fine," I said and started up the stairs.

"Happy birthday Emma, I love you."

"God help me Michael, I love you too." When I got up to my room I called Allie.

"Are you ok?" she asked when she picked up.

"I will be fine, just exhausted all of a sudden," I said with a small laugh.

She laughed, "So where is he now?" I knew she was asking because she thought I would have let him back upstairs already.

"Sleeping on the couch," I said.

"I'm proud of you Emma. I kind of want to punch the prick in the face you know?"

"I do, but please don't. I am going to try and work through this with him."

"I figured you would. You know how I feel about his worthiness." She said with a laugh.

I giggled, "Allie you don't think anyone is worthy of me, same as I feel about you."

"That's right and some putz who makes a speech like that, really doesn't"

"Al, please."

"I'm sorry, I just..."

"I know. I love him though; I have to at least give him another chance. You don't really believe he thinks those things do you?"

"If he does he doesn't know you at all. No I don't believe he thinks what he said is true. I don't know what his problem is, maybe it was the whiskey. But that doesn't make it ok."

"No it doesn't"

"And he has to do a lot of groveling," she said with a snicker.

"Yes he does," I said laughing a little now.

"Ok then, but I want it known I am not a fan."

"I know."

"And that I love you like a fat kid loves cake."

I burst into laughter. "Well I love you like a fat kid loves and all you can eat ice cream bar. As a fat kid, I don't like cake."

"You're a dork," she said.

"Agreed. Oh speaking of dorks, you told you brother?"

"You knew I would, you can't even tell me you were surprised he called?"

"Nope, can't say I was."

"Ok go to bed old lady, I will see you for dinner tomorrow night."

"Good night Allie."

"Good night Emma Grace and happy birthday."

I hung up and went to sleep. When I woke up Michael made me breakfast and we talked for hours about what happened. He promised it would never happen again, it didn't. For the next nine months things were better, not perfect, but nothing is ever perfect right? "I'm sorry" became Michael's favorite saying. Not because he would say anything terrible, but because he was always canceling dates. When I did see him, it was always great and it always made me happy, but it sometimes got a little lonely.

CHAPTER ELEVEN

Allie went on hating him, of course. Every time he would call and cancel something she got a little more annoyed. But they were civil to one another. Brandon still emailed me all the time talking on the phone was still a little difficult with all of his traveling. He seemed relatively happy for me. "Are you happy?" he asked me on a rare phone call.

I paused. "Yeah I'm happy." I said

"You paused." He pointed out

"No I didn't," I said, knowing completely that I had.

"My sister hates him." He said plainly, which made me laugh. "Why is that funny?"

"Because you must know I already know that. Your sister doesn't hide her emotions as well as other people in her family." Why I was trying to provoke him I wasn't sure.

His voice came back like ice and it made me shiver. "You should talk." He hissed.

"Brandon, I..."

His voice was softer this time. "I'm sorry." He whispered. I could tell it was for more than just his harsh words and it made me want to cry. "I miss you." He said after a long pause.

"I miss you too." I said holding back the tears.

"I am happy if you're happy." He said finally.

"Thank you." I said. "Are you happy?" I asked.

"Sometimes," He paused. "Sometimes not so much, but it's not bad. I am getting to see the world."

"I am proud of you."

"Thanks that means a lot. But I have to get going ok. Will you call me tomorrow? I would really like to talk to you again. I miss your voice."

There was a long pause before I answered. "Of course" I said. I had gotten over my crush on Brandon a while ago, and I was truly happy with the way life was turning out, but I couldn't survive if he wasn't in my life at all.

"Good. I miss you Emma Grace, you're still the most beautiful girl I know." Before I could respond he was gone. Sad and a little infuriated I called his sister.

"Your brother will eventually send me to a mental institution." I said when she answered.

Her laugh was so loud I had to pull the phone from my ear. "What did he say?" she asked.

"That I was still the most beautiful girl he knows."

"That makes you mentally unstable?" she asked

"Allie!!!" My screech made her laugh harder.

"Ok, ok I can see your point. But your happy with Shitbrick right?" she asked sounding even more amused.

"Please stop calling him that."

"Ok you're happy with ..." she seemed to almost choke. "Michael right?" she hated saying his name. They cared less and less for each other since my birthday and the only reason they put up with each other at all was because they both loved me so much. I should have felt guilty, but I didn't

I paused again. What was with all the pausing today? Freaking Brandon. "Yes, I am" I finally answered.

"Well then, that is all that matters. Take a deep breath, he just wants to feel things out and make sure you're happy. He would never do anything to hurt you on purpose Emm."

"I know," I answered. I knew that, but it didn't make the fact that he thought that any less painful. "I think I am going to take a shower and head to bed. I will see you tomorrow."

"Ok girl, stop worrying. Calm down, take a deep breath and maybe a shot of vodka." She laughed again

"Good night Allie." I said and hung up. I took a shower and went to bed trying not to think about Brandon at all. I drifted off into a dreamless sleep.

When I woke up the next morning I heard someone out in my kitchen. It was a Saturday and it was only about 6am, far, far too early to be awake. But I was suddenly, as I had no idea who could be in my home. I picked up my phone, ready to dial 911 if I needed and a baseball bat and tiptoed down the stairs. I poked my head around the corner. I calmed down immediately when I saw that it was Michael. When I snuck up behind him and put my arms around his waist he jumped. "Holy shit Emma, you scared me half to death." The look on his face was angry and annoyed.

It irritated me and I lashed back. "You're the one who snuck into MY house ass hole." I went and sat down in a kitchen chair. His face softened and then he took in my appearance. "What?" I said. "You woke me up."

He smiled and looked over my nightwear again. Wonder woman panties and a t-shirt. He laughed. "I love when you wear the wonder woman ones." He grinned. I laughed at his horny boyish grin. "Well now seems like as good a time as any, seeing as though you are wearing my favorite outfit."

"Good a time as any for what?"

As the words came out of my mouth he was getting down on one knee and pulling something from his back pocket. "Oh my god, oh my god." Was the only thought racing through my mind. He opened the box revealing a huge oval diamond, with a gold band. I'll get to my thoughts on the ring later. Then he said. "Emma Peters, would you do me the honor of spending the rest of your life with me?" I stared at him. This was nothing like I had ever dreamed this moment would be. I had wanted it to be at Fenway Park, not in my kitchen in my undies. And the ring was nothing I had ever mentioned liking, it was something I knew he thought was flashy and he could show off to people. It was the wrong place, the wrong time, the wrong ring and the wrong…. But I pushed all those thoughts aside and focused on the fact that the man I loved was asking me to marry him.

"Yes" I whispered. "Yes of course I'll marry you."

As soon as the words were out of my mouth I felt a sudden sense of panic, but I just choked it up to nerves about getting engaged. Michael seemed elated. He picked me up and spun me around kissing me. I giggled in his arms, and his grin just grew bigger.

"Emma you have made me the happiest man on earth." He said finally putting me down and kissing me; I just smiled up at him. "We should tell people we should tell everyone!" he exclaimed.

I laughed at his enthusiasm. "Can I put some clothes on first maybe?"

He looked me over again and then smirked at me. "Not till I take advantage of what you have on now first."

I giggled and he took my hand and led me upstairs to the bedroom. "I love you Emma." He said and smiled at me as he laid me on the bed. "You are so beautiful and smart and funny and you have made me the happiest man on the planet right now. I could not ask for anything more."

I smiled at him, butterflies were jumping in my stomach, Michael hadn't been this sappy and sweet in a long time, and I rather liked it. "I love you too. I am very happy." I said and kissed him. He smiled at me and kissed me hungrily. It was soft and gentle and everything I loved it to be. This day, our engagement had made him my lovely Michael.

A bit later we were lying in bed, "I have to go to work soon." He said looking at me and making a face that was half sad and half apologetic.

I pouted at him; "Michael it's a Saturday and we just got engaged. Can you please just stay here in bed with me today?" I kissed his neck.

"I have to go in today so I can have a free day tomorrow." he looked at me; I leaned in and kissed his jaw. He chuckled, "but I don't have to go now." and he kissed me again.

When Michael finally left to go to the office, I called Allie. "Hi." I said. I couldn't tell if my voice sounded excited or completely petrified.

"Hello." She said sounding more than a bit suspicious. "What's going on?" she asked

"Nothing," I answered too quickly

"Liar!!" she snickered on the other end. "Emma I have known you for almost eighteen years. You don't think you can actually lie to me do you?"

I sighed, she was right; no matter how good I was at lying I could never lie to her, or her brother, they both always saw right through me. "Well um... Michael came over this morning and asked me something."

"Ok"

"He asked me to..."

"Did you say yes?" she interrupted me.

"I did."

"I see. Well then, I am happy if you are happy."

"Convincing," I snickered. This was actually better than the reaction I was expecting.

"What do you want me to say Emm. He seems to make you happy and he seems to love you, so I am happy if you are happy."

"But you're not happy."

She sighed. "I am happy, I am not ecstatic, but you didn't really expect me to be did you?"

"No this is actually better than the reaction I had pictured in my head."

She laughed loudly. "Emma I love you, you're my sister for all intent and purposes. Truly if you are happy, then so I am."

"Thank you."

"No problem. Are you going to tell him or should I?" she asked and I knew immediately whom she was referring to. "I think you should, but you know I can't make any promises that I won't give him hints about it. Just so he is a little prepared."

"I should tell him." I almost whispered. "I don't know why this is so hard. I mean he kissed me over 11 years ago and never since. Why is it so hard to tell him I am happy with someone else?"

"I can't tell you that Emm, you need to figure it out on your own." She paused thoughtfully I expect hoping some revelation to come to me, when it didn't she continued. "Shall I put on my Maid of Honor hat and come over?"

"Yes please and thank you. Or just come over leave the hat at home for now."

When we hung up I went and took a shower and got dressed. I sat down on the couch with my phone in hand and dialed. I could feel my hand shaking when I finished, but his voice mail picked up automatically.

"Hi this is Brandon, I can't answer my phone right now, leave a message if you're my family or well you know, and I will call you back. If not your efforts may be fruitless but try anyway, you might catch me on a good day." BEEP.

"Um... Hi B. I don't know if you phone died or what, but could you call me back Hun. I have some news for you. Talk to you soon. Oh this is Emma by the way, in case you didn't know" I closed the phone thinking that I may actually be a moron for even worrying about this. I mean if he wanted to be with me he had plenty of opportunity before I met Michael. I was being a bit full of myself, I thought, to think he would be upset about my getting married. I decided I was being silly and got off the couch just as the doorbell rung.

When I opened the door, Allie was standing there with a huge grin on her face. "What?" I asked looking at her. "Why are you grinning like that?"

"It's a surprise, I can't tell you. But I have the feeling you are going to love it." She grinned wider.

"Tell me!" I demanded laughing. I loved surprises but if I knew one was coming I hated waiting.

"Emma Grace, if I tell you what it is it will ruin the surprise. I am just sorry I won't be there to see your face when it comes." I looked at her strangely and she just smirked again. I decided I wasn't going to get anything from her so I dropped it. She came into the house and immediately took my left hand in hers. She inspected the ring with a displeased look on her face. I laughed because I knew she was thinking the same thing I was. "Um… it's nice." She said trying to smile.

I laughed, "No it isn't, well it is, but for someone else ya know?"

"Yes." She said relieved to see I was thinking the same as her.

"Sometimes he doesn't listen very well." I said shrugging.

"Or at all," I heard her say under her breath but she looked up and smiled at me. "It must be worth a small fortune. It's a big diamond anyway."

I made a face at the ring. "Yeah it's pretty." I said looking down at it and shrugging again. "If his biggest mistake is picking out the wrong kind of ring, then I am still a pretty lucky girl." I smiled at her, her returning smiled looked worried.

"Sure" was her only response.

The rest of the night went on without talking about wedding or the ring that was on my hand. When she left, Michael came over. He was in a foul mood, which irritated me. And I glared at him "what's your problem?" I growled at him. He turned and looked at me, surprised by my tone and his face softened immediately.

He smiled at me, pushing a stray hair out of my face and tracing my frown with his finger. "I'm sorry baby." He started. "I had a really bad day, this stupid deposition is killing me, but that isn't your fault. This should be a happy day. Today is the first day I will be spending the rest of my life with you." I smiled at his cheesiness and he took me into his arms and kissed me walking towards the bedroom.

When we woke up in the morning he was grinning at me. "What are you so happy about?" I said laughing. "You're even less of a morning person than I am."

He chuckled. "Its 8" he said smiling. This was late for Michael.

"Ah." I said and pulled the blankets around me tighter. "You still didn't explain why you are so happy this morning."

"Because I cleared my whole schedule today, I am taking you on a special date."

"Oh?" I asked curiously. The last time Michael took me on a "special date" he took a train to New York and took a tour of Wall Street, not my idea of a good time.

He laughed; I imagine because he knew what I was thinking. "I promise it will be an Emma approved date. Now come and take a shower." And with that he lifted me out of the bed.

When we were dressed I looked at him expectantly. "Well?" I said

"Patience, you're awful feisty" and he laughed.

"I'm curious is all; I want to know what you think an Emma approved date is."

"Do you think I don't know you very well?" he asked raising one eyebrow with a smirk on his face.

I laughed, "You're really cute when you look at me like that."

"Changing the subject are you?"

I giggled. "No, I know you know me, it's just you don't always enjoy what I like to do, so you don't do it."

He laughed, which I was glad I thought he would get angry. "You're right, I'm sorry about that. But you're going to be my wife now; I have to keep you happy forever." He smiled and kissed me.

"Interesting, so I will get my lovely Michael more?"

"Ninety nine point nine percent of the time," He grinned

"I'll take it." I said laughing. "Can we go now, the suspense is killing me.

He laughed again, "you're like a little kid sometimes, and it's adorable." I grinned at him widely and he chuckled. "Come on goof ball."

He took my hand and we walked out to the car. A few minutes later he pulled up in front of IHOP. "Oh," I said with a smiled.

He laughed again, "stay here, I'll be right back."

"What?" I exclaimed

"We're not eating it here."

"But how do you…"

He cut me off with his laughter, "Emma my love, I know exactly what you want." I pouted slightly and he chuckled as he closed the door and ran inside.

When he came back out and got in the car with the bag, I went to open it. "Hey," he laughed, "not yet. Just put it in the back seat."

"You're kind of mean." I said but couldn't help smiling. "I'm starving."

"You can eat soon enough." He said. He pulled around the corner and got me a coffee from my favorite coffee shop.

I sipped it smiling. "How long have you been planning this day?" I asked him

He grinned at me. "I was actually going to ask you to marry me today." He said. "But I just couldn't wait once I already had the ring in my hand." He smiled at me and I laughed. "Plus you know what the wonder woman undies do to me."

"You're too adorable." I said to him and laughed again. "Ok so can I have a hint as to where we are going?"

"Nope," He smirked

"There better be a good excuse for you waking me up at 8am on a Sunday." I crossed my arms across my chest and attempted to pout but I couldn't help but smile.

"Such a child sometimes," He laughed and took my hand as he drove. He got on the highway and I looked at him confused he just smiled. When I noticed he was getting off at the aquarium exit I

started bouncing in the seat. "This is just the start."
He said smiling.

"Oh, oh, oh, I love the aquarium." He chuckled and
I leaned across the seat and kissed his cheek.

We sat in front of the aquarium and ate breakfast;
he got me stuffed French toast, my favorite. Then
we walked around the aquarium for a few hours and
I got to stare at turtles. He was sweet and charming
the whole time and he didn't complain once. When
we were leaving I asked him, "so when were you
going to ask me to marry you?"

"When we were outside eating breakfast," He
smiled.

"This has been a really nice day babe." I kissed his
hand.

"Well thanks to my dad it's not over. I called him
last night to tell him and he gave me something as a
present for you."

"What is it?" my eyes widened. He reached in his
pocket and pulled out Bob's season tickets to the
Red Sox. "Oh, oh."

He laughed again, "I can't understand your
obsession with the sport, but he thought you would
like them."

When he was still talking I was already dialing. "Bob, thank you so much, I am so excited."

"You deserve it Emma. Have a Fenway frank for me."

"Will do boss, see you tomorrow. I love you Bob."

He chuckled, "I love you too dear. Don't let my son complain too much."

"Oh, I won't." I said and winked at Michael. "I am obsessed because it great." I answered his earlier comment. "Fenway is my happy place, my Disney World if you will. When was the last time you went to a game?"

He smiled his wickedly brilliant smiled that always sent my heart racing. "Our second date." He said

"Oh yeah, that was a great date." I said giggling. I leaned over and kissed him, "we should totally have a repeat of that night."

"I was thinking the same thing." He said kissing me again. "Come on, we don't want to be late for the game." He smirked.

"No we definitely don't want to do that." I said jumping to my feet. He laughed at me because he had been kidding and he knew that I was completely serious. Bob's tickets were amazing. We sat in the front row, first base line about thirty seats from the dugout. It was a great game, Tampa Bay, always a good time. I screamed and yelled and sang sweet Caroline all while Michael smiled at me, he did actually sing though, and I was impressed. "Wow!" I said to him when he looked at me with a big goofy grin.

He laughed, "It's a combination of your infectious enthusiasm and all the beer." He grinned again.

I giggled, "Whatever it is, I like it." And I kissed him. When the game was over we took the train to his house. It was easier to park the car there and ride the green line to Kenmore. The whole way back to Park Street I was rubbing his back as we both giggled like little kids. When we got in the elevator to his building he pushed me up against the wall and kissed me. I struggled to un-tuck his shirt from his pants. He chuckled then scooped me up into his arms as the doors opened on his floor. He laughed as he tried to open his door, hold me and kiss me all at the same time. Remarkably he managed to get the door opened.

Without putting me down he started undressing me as he walked to the bedroom. "I'm impressed with this talent you suddenly have." I said and kissed his neck

He chuckled "I need you to be naked as soon as possible." By the time we reached the bedroom I was. He pulled off his shirt and climbed into the bed with me. I unbuckled his pants and pulled them off then moved back up his body to kiss him. We made love for what seemed liked hours.

"Wow!" he said rolling over. I just giggled. "I can't remember the last time it was that good. I mean it's always amazing." He said turning to grin at me. I rolled my eyes at him. "But that, that was like honeymoon stage good."

I laughed and wrapped my arms around him. "I'm hungry. You want me to make you something?" I asked

"I would love that." He said kissing me.

"What would you like?" I said getting up and walking to the kitchen, he didn't answer so I turned around and saw he had been watching me walk away with a smiled on his face. "See something you like?" I asked giggling.

He chuckled and shook his head I started to pout when he said, "Nope, I see something I love though." Then he grinned widely.

"You're such a cheese ball." I said giggling. "I love it."

"I love you." he said

"I love you too. Now what do you want to eat?" I asked again pulling on my panties.

"We could order in Thai." He said with a smiled, "then you could come back to bed till they get here."

"Hmmm" I said as I stood in the doorway trying to appear as though it was a hard decision to make. "Ok." I said and ran across the room jumping on the bed. He chuckled and kissed me as he dialed to phone. We didn't need a menu, we ordered from the Thai take out place so often we almost didn't have to tell them what we wanted.

"Can I have an order for delivery?" Michael said into the phone. "Can I have two orders of cashew chicken…?"

"Oh sticky rice and spring rolls oh and get me some Thai tea." I said to him.

He chuckled again and gave the man my list of food. I bit my lip and smiled. He grinned at me and pulled me to him to kiss me. "He said we have thirty minutes." He said with one eyebrow raised and a smirk on his face.

I giggled, "You're like a horny teenager today." I said, "What brought all of this on? Not that I'm complaining because I love it."

"I just realized that sometimes I take you for granted. I'm not always to best man and I think you get to raw end of the deal. When you said yes, I could see you had hesitation."

"No I didn't." I said, but remembered the feeling of panic when I said it.

"Emma, I'm not stupid." He said, but he was smiling. "I know that I am a jerk sometimes. I don't blame you at all for having reservations about marrying me. But I want to be a better man for you; I want to be the man you deserve. There is no one like you on this earth and I am not about to give you up without a fight." I smiled and kissed him, which effectively ended the conversation until the food came. I hoped that Michael was serious about his change. I wanted so badly to have my lovely Michael all the time. If today was any indications of the future we would have together, then I had no reason to think I would be anything less than blissfully happy.

CHAPTER TWELVE

When I woke up for work in the morning he was gone. There was a note with a carnation on the pillow beside me.

Sorry I had to leave so early my love, I will see you tonight

Michael.

I rolled my eyes. "Ok" I thought, "he doesn't know my favorite flower either." I hate carnations but it's the thought that counts I told myself.

When I got to work that morning, the small numbers of women were all buzzing about some gorgeous man that was in Bob's office. I paid no attention to them and went into my own. My assistant followed me in "let me see that?" she demanded my hand. Margo had been my assistant for about four years since I was promoted to manager. She was lovely, but a bit pushy. "Well." She tapped her foot impatiently. I sighed and gave her my hand. "Oh, oh it's lovely." I smiled at her and she rolled her eyes at my reaction. "I promise." She said I laughed, which made her smile and she left then poked her head back in. "you need to head over to Bob's office and check out the bronze god he has in there. Wowie!!" and she was gone again. I laughed and sat down at my desk.

About 20 minutes later I got a call from Bob to come to his office with the layout for a project I had been working on. All of the women watched me as I walked, because the man was apparently still in Bob's office and I was the only one who hadn't seen him yet. When I walked in, Bob smiled at me and I looked at the back of the mysterious person's head. Without having him turn around I knew who it was immediately. "Brandon." I said it as if I was simply breathing.

He turned to face me. His smile was alarmingly beautiful. He came bounding across the room as I beamed at him, picked me up and spun me around. "Hello Emma Grace." He said. I heard comments coming from outside of the office but I ignored them. "I missed you," he whispered in my ear.

"You have no idea." I whispered back, hugging him tighter. "What are you doing here?" I asked no longer whispering.

He put me down and smiled at me, turning to Bob who was smiling at both of us. "I just hired him." "His portfolio is quite impressive." A smug look came across Brandon's face and I rolled my eyes. "You can't do everything all on your own Emma so when he showed it to me, and then I found out you two know each other I knew he should work here before he goes and works for one of our competitors. Plus I think you two will work well together." It was then I became convinced that the world was out to get me. "Brandon have you heard that Emma is going to be my daughter-in-law?" Bob asked, I could swear I saw him frowning as he said it. Which scared me because I thought I was already like his daughter? I was woken from my mini panic attack by Brandon's words.

"Really?" he said feigning interest but I saw him wince slightly. I put my hand on his arm and his took it in his hand squeezing it. He was handling it well. I had worried about nothing. He winked at me and then I knew why.

"Allie!!" I said through my teeth. He smiled down at me and nodded laughing slightly and squeezing my hand again.

"I am a lucky man." Bob said smiling again, forever ceasing my panic.

"Well that is just fantastic!!" Brandon exclaimed with a lot of false enthusiasm, that Bob apparently did not catch. I nudged him. "What?" he mouthed to me smiling. "I'm glad I came home then. Now I can make sure that Emma has the happiness she deserves." He smirked but didn't look at me. He was looking at Bob who smirked back at him. Some plan was in order and I was suddenly annoyed I wasn't in on it, even though it was obviously about me.

"You two are irritating me." I said forcing a smile. I looked at both of them. "Do you want me to make introductions? There are 5 women out there waiting to simply hear you speak. Do you need us for anything else Bob?"

"No dear. Go introduce him and show him around. Plus I am sure you have a lot to talk about." They were both smirking again. I rolled my eyes at them and walked from the office, Brandon would not let go of my left hand.

"Can we go in your office and talk about this thing before I meet people?" he asked. I looked at him and saw he was making a displeased face at the ring. I laughed at him.

"You are so much like your sister sometimes it scares me." I squeezed his hand and he smiled a bit. "Speaking of your sister I think I am going to have to kill her. I hope you won't miss her terribly."

"Nah, I'll get by. I have you." He smiled. I smiled back shaking my head.

"I'm introducing you first. It's rude not to. Then we can go in my office and you can tell me all about the fact that it is the complete wrong ring for me and all the other stuff."

"Fair enough" he said

I walked him around the office introducing him to everyone. Most of the women tried to flirt, which Brandon did not even seem to notice. He seemed anxious to get the introductions over so we could speak alone. When I finally got around to introducing him to Margo she looked at us curiously.

"It's nice to meet you Brandon. I have heard a lot about you. I had not expected you to be so handsome though. I think things are going to get interesting around here." She said and winked at me.

"It's nice to meet you too Margo." He smiled and looked at me. "And I hope it is." She giggled and went back to her desk.

Yup, the whole world is out to get me. "Did you come here to torture me?" I asked him as I closed my office door behind us.

"Do you really think that I would do that?" he asked, all trace of his smile gone.

"No." I answered him and looked away embarrassed at my question.

He chuckled now. "I came back because for one it was time. I can't be a bum forever. And two, I missed my family, I missed you and I want to make sure that you really are happy."

I smiled up at him. "I am." I said

"Good. But can we talk about that thing on your finger?"

I laughed again. "It's awful isn't it? Well it's nice, but…"

"It's so not you." He smiled. "Can we talk about that please?"

"Let's call your sister first. I think she might want to get in on this conversation too. Plus I have a few choice words for her. She was supposed to let me tell you."

"Oh come on, you knew she would tell me. My sister can't keep a secret to save her life. Plus she thought it might be easier if she told me before you did."

I looked at him confused. "That's silly." I said. "Was it?"

He laughed "Not sure yet. I think I have to meet this guy and see if he is good enough for you. I'm sure he's not, but we can see if he at least comes close." He stopped to smile at me. "Allie really does hate his guts."

"That's because Allie has the same mentality as you. She doesn't think anyone is good enough. Or well almost anyone." I looked at him quickly, he looked like he was about to say something but I kept talking. "Michael is a little hard to take sometimes. He's a bit too intense. Short temper, but he's not a bad guy. He's good to me."

He smiled half-heartedly. "Well then, if you're happy then I am happy."

I groaned. "Seriously do the two of you read from the same supportive friend handbook? I feel like I am having the same conversation I had with your sister yesterday."

He laughed. "We both love you. She's been your best friend for a long time; you're like a sister to her."

"And you?" I asked wondering if I wasn't trying to torture myself at that point.

"You're my best friend." He grinned. "I thank my stupid fifteen year old self for that every day. If I hadn't... well you know, then you might still just think of me as some annoying kid and I would have missed knowing the most wonderful person I have ever met." He looked at me and I had tears in my eyes. His face grew worried. "Oh, oh I'm sorry, what did I say?"

I smiled at him and laughed, "Nothing that is just so sweet." Relief washed across his face. "I would not have survived most of this life if it wasn't for the two of you." I smacked him in the arm. "Don't you ever leave for six years without coming home again. I don't think I could bear it now that I have you here."

"I'm not going anywhere." He said and wrapped his arms around me.

"You better not." I whispered, and hugged him tighter. When he stopped hugging me I went over to my desk and dialed his sister's number.

When the phone picked up she didn't even say hello. "Surprise!" she answered.

"You're a dead woman." I said coldly

"I tried Emm I swear I did. I was only going to give him hints, it's not my fault he's a good guesser. You had to know he is super intelligent, after all he is my little brother." She giggled. "I am a little annoyed she got to see you first though. You just dropped your stuff in my living room and took off." She said to Brandon .

"She's cuter than you are." He said and winked at me. I could feel my face flush. "Did you tell Mom and dad?"

"Yeah but they are in Hawaii right now. Mom is ecstatic she can't wait to see you."

"Ok people back to the matter at hand." I said.

"You're ring is ugly, you hate carnations, I hate your fiancée, but I'm happy if you're happy." Allie said

"Ditto," Brandon concurred. "Except the part about hating your fiancée, I don't know him yet; I will wait to pass judgment."

"It won't take long." Allie said

"Hello, I am sitting right here."

"So did he ask you at Fenway?" Brandon asked.

"Um…" I started

"No he didn't." Allie spat. "He asked her in her kitchen when she was in her undies."

"He what?" Brandon looked at me.

"Oh knock it off, both of you." I was beginning to get annoyed. "It's just fantastic that you are both together and can gang up on me like old times. Yes ok it's the wrong ring, it was the wrong place a lot about it is wrong, but he asked and he loves me and I love him so drop it ok."

"I'm sorry" Brandon said

"Me too" said Allie. "We just want you to have everything you want. We want to make absolute sure that he's good enough for you."

"Will there ever be anyone who is?"

"No." Brandon said and smiled halfheartedly. I smiled at him and he chuckled.

"Ok tonight we are going out to dinner to catch up." Allie said

"I can't tonight, how about tomorrow night?" I answered.

Allie groaned, "Ok fine, looks like it's just you and me tonight little brother."

"Fantastic." He said sarcastically and winked at me.

"Ok I am hanging up on you now, I am still furious with you."

"Oh you sound furious." She said laughing.

"Oh shut up. Good bye I will see you tomorrow night."

"Bye. I'll see you tomorrow. See you soon little brother, I've missed you."

"I missed you too." He said and I hung up on her. "She didn't actually tell me you know." He said looking at me now.

"What did she say exactly?"

"She said, 'I have to tell you something about Emma and Michael' and the way she said it didn't tell me that you had broken up. So I decided I didn't need to find myself anymore and I came home. I wanted to make sure you were happy."

"I'm happy." I said with a half smile

"All the time?"

"Is anyone happy all the time?"

"They should be."

"I think that's a bit unrealistic don't you?" I frowned. "If I waited for someone who made me happy all the time I would be waiting forever." I looked at his face, which looked sad now. I didn't like that. "I missed you so much, you know that?"

He smiled, "Good because I missed you more."

We spent the rest of the afternoon talking. He told me about all of the places he had been and all the things he had seen. I looked through his portfolio it really was quite impressive.

"So tell me," I said after I had finished looking at his portfolio, "you can clearly work anywhere with this portfolio, why did you pick here?"

"Because I have never heard anyone talk about the place that they work with such love as you do." He said with a smile.

"I do?" I asked almost embarrassed now.

He smiled, "yes you talk about this place like it is some kind of paradise, and you talk about Bob like he is another father to you. I liked that, I like that this place makes you happy. I just wanted to be part of that, and I thought if I was going to come back to civilization and get a job, I should get a job that there is a pretty good chance that I will be happy."

"I do love this place. I have never had a job that I loved so much. I get to do what I love and I have a lot of creative license."

"Bob told me. He seems like a really nice guy, and he clearly loves you. If his son is anything like him, then I am sure he and I will get along famously."

I laughed, mostly because I knew that Michael and his father could not be less alike. Michael thought his father was too much of a dreamer. They had little in common, but Michael was still a good man. We spent the remainder of the day going over some upcoming projects he would be helping me with and just trying to catch up as much as we could. It was a nice day and I was so happy to have him home again.

CHAPTER THIRTEEN

When I got home that night I started dinner for Michael and me. I couldn't stop smiling. I didn't realize how happy I was to have Brandon home until I wasn't with him anymore. I was singing to myself when Michael came in.

"Honey I'm home." He called out then chuckled.

I giggled, "Hi Hun." I said. I was trying without result to wipe the ever-widening grin off my face.

"You look very happy tonight," he said leaning around me and taking a mushroom off the cutting board. "What's up?" he asked grinning himself.

"Guess what your father did today?" I said

"What did my father do today?" he said chuckling. He never was one for guessing he just wanted to answers.

"He hired Brandon Jacobs." I said grinning wider. I needed to stop; my face was starting to hurt.

"Who?" he asked, slightly disinterested now that he knew it had nothing to do with him.

I rolled my eyes at him. "Brandon Jacobs as in Allie Jacobs and in Allie's little brother Brandon." I said looking at his face for some recognition. And then I saw it and he smirked.

"Ah, that Brandon," He said nodding. "I thought he was off in Europe somewhere?"

"He was. He just came home."

"That's convenient." He said. "That's an awful big smile you have." He pointed out trying his best to smile. I grinned even wider when I realized that Michael was actually jealous. Normally he was far too full of himself to feel threatened by anyone.

"Are you jealous?" I asked grinning and turning from the counter to poke him.

He frowned. "Does that bother you?"

"No, quite to opposite I think it's rather sexy. But why are you jealous?"

"I've never seen you smile like that for anyone but me." He said grinning. "You think it's sexy that I am jealous?"

"I do it's a new side of you. I've never seen Michael Mackay threatened by anyone." I wrapped my arms around his neck and he pulled me into his arms.

"I could pick a fight with him, give you the full effect." He said chuckling.

"Now that, I would not like at all," I said frowning at him.

He smiled and kissed me. "I wouldn't do that, especially now that I know it would make you unhappy. And I don't want to do that." He grinned and kissed my neck. I giggled. "So when do I get to meet this boy?" he asked kissing the other side of my neck.

He had sat me down on the counter now in front of him beside the chopped vegetables. "Well we are going out for dinner tomorrow night, Brandon, Allie and Me. But you don't have to come if you..." I interrupted myself with more giggling as he kissed my chin and ears. "If you don't stop I am going to burn dinner."

"We can order out." He said as he leaned over to turn off the stove then picked me up and carried me into the bedroom.

The next morning when I woke up Michael was still there. When I opened my eyes he was staring at me. I could feel a huge smile coming across my face. "Good morning." I said to him. "What's the special occasion?" he knew that I meant he was still there and hadn't left for the office. He chuckled and my smiled grew wider.

"I love when that smile is for me." He said leaning over to kiss me.

I smiled and kissed him quickly then got up to go brush my teeth. "So what's the special occasion?" I asked again.

"I called in the office and told them I would be in at nine like everyone else." I could hear the smile in his voice even though I couldn't see his face.

I poked my head out of the bathroom, toothbrush still in my mouth, "Seriously?" I asked. "Again, what's the occasion?"

"I just wanted to spend the morning with you. I don't get to spend enough morning with you."

"No you don't." I said matter of factly. "I am loving this new leaf you have turned over. I have to say, you are making me the happiest girl in the world."

"That's my goal." He said getting up and coming over to the bathroom door.

"Is it now?" I said wrapping my arms around his waist. By now I had finished brushing my teeth.

"It is, and to show you how much I want to be good for you, I am going to take you and your friends to dinner."

114

"Baby you don't have to do that."

"I know that love, but I haven't exactly been nice to Allie either. I would like to make it up to her, and make a good impression on Brandon."

"Who are you and what have you done with my Fiancée?" I giggled. "Did you have like a near death experience or something? What brought on this revelation?" I asked him. His behavior, although great, was actually starting to frighten me a bit.

He chuckled, "Sort of. You could say that seeing the hesitation in your eyes before you said yes was kind of a wakeup call. I spent the whole night trying to figure out why you would have to take any time to think about it. Then I started remembering all the things I've said and done. How awful I am to your friends and when I make you spend time with my stuffy friends. You're too full of life for those people." He smiled at me.

I jumped into his arms and kissed him. "I have to take a shower." I said walking into the bathroom. He nodded and stepped back into the bedroom. "Aren't you coming?" I said grinning. That was all the invitation he needed.

When I got to work I was about five minutes late, which I never am. "Did we have a good morning?" Margo said as I walked past her with a huge grin on my face.

"You could say it was a good morning." I winked. "Sorry I'm late."

"First time in almost eight years, I think you can be forgiven. Brandon is in your office."

"Why?" I asked confused.

She laughed, "I don't ask questions when men that beautiful tell me they are going to sit in your office." I rolled my eyes at her. "If only my husband could be that fine."

"Your husband is gorgeous." I said which was completely true. Someone as beautiful as Margo was destined to be with someone just as beautiful.

She brightened up, "Yeah he is." She said smiling. I rolled my eyes again and walked into my office.

"You're late." He said grinning when I walked through the door. I just smiled at him. "Ah someone had a good morning." He chuckled but there wasn't a lot of joy behind the laugh.

"Sorry about that. What's up?" I went and sat down at my desk.

"I was wondering if you wanted to get breakfast. I am so in the mood for IHOP."

I smiled, "I am always in the mood for that."

"Me too," Margo called out. "I'll go get it if you want."

"Does she always listen to your conversations?" Brandon asked me.

I laugh and nodded. "I want stuffed French toast."

"Oh, that's so surprising." Margo said sarcastically. We gave her our order and she left.

"So you seem really happy today." He said without smiling.

I just grinned at him, which made the corners of his mouth turn up slightly. "I am having a good day." I said. "Oh Michael wants to take us all out to dinner."

"Really?" he grinned. "Allie will find that interesting."

I rolled my eyes. "He said he realized he's been a jerk and he wants to be better. He said when I hesitated before saying yes; he realized he had to change to keep me."

"You hesitated?" he asked trying miserably to fight a smile.

"Just for a second," I said looking at him sternly.

"Why?" he had completely given up trying not to smile.

"For the exact reasons he thinks he needs to change. I love that man, when he is good, he is almost perfect but when he's bad... well he's really bad."

"Does he actually know you have named his two personalities?" he chuckled

I smiled, "I have only named one, the good one. My lovely Michael," I laughed. "Yes he knows, whenever he is goody say, 'oh my lovely Michael came for a visit.' Sometimes he laughs. Sometimes I lose him, but either way I've gotten to the point where I don't hide when he annoys me."

"Well that makes me happy," he said smiling.

I laughed and shook my head. "So where should we make him take us?"

"Hmm" he said then got up and started dialing my phone. I would have been annoyed if I didn't know he was calling Allie.

"Hello, Allie Jacobs consulting how can I help you?"

"Michael wants to take us all to dinner tonight and Emma wants to know where we should make him take us." He said

118

"Top of the hub," She said snickering.

"Oh please." I said. "Can we be at least a little reasonable? How about the Inn?"

"Of course you pick your favorite place," she said.

"Don't act like you don't love it too," I answered back.

"Ok fine, I love it too, yeah let's go there!" she said.

Brandon made a face as if he wasn't sure about our choice, "I've never been there before, is it any good."

"Delicious!!" I said. "They have about eighty seven kinds of cheesecake. And lobster and it's on the beach."

"Well the Inn it is then." Allie said. "Around seven?"

"Perfect." I answered.

"Alright see you at your house around six thirty. I have to actually go do work now. I have a bride who is having pictures taken of her and her fiancée in a morgue today. Yay fun," she said, her voice dripping with sarcasm. "I will see you tonight." and she hung up.

Brandon smiled at me then got up. "Where are you off to?" I asked him

"I have my own office."

"Doesn't seem like it." I smiled at him and giggled.

He rolled his eyes at me, "well I'll be back when Margo come in with breakfast," and he left the room.

The rest of the day flew by. I called Michael and let him know the plan for the night. He was excited to meet Brandon. I was a little skeptical about his eagerness but I let it go in the hopes that this was just another one of his ways of trying to be a better. We agreed he would meet the three of us at the restaurant at seven.

"I'm excited baby." He said before hanging up.

"So am I. I want them to see the Michael I have for the last few days."

"I'll make sure I bring him with me," he said chuckling. "I love you, I will see you tonight."

"I love you too, see you then."

When work was over Brandon, Allie and I met at my house so I could get changed.

"Why do you need to change your clothes, you look nice?" Allie said.

I smiled at her, "Thank you dear, but I spilt maple syrup all over my shirt." I said pulling my jacket open. Brandon chuckled next to me. "Why are you laughing, you are so paying to have this dry cleaned you know." I said trying to sound angry but unable to stop the giggle that escaped my lips

"What did you do?" Allie said to her brother smiling

"I may have smacked her arm when she why trying to pour the syrup." He grinned

"He's very mature." I said. I walked into my room and pulled on a different shirt. "Ok ready to go?" I said walking out into the living room. "Remember, he's making an effort here, so please at least give him that chance." I said mostly to Allie.

"If he has been as good as you tell me, then that will be no problem." She grinned. I could tell she didn't believe he had, but she was willing to be good.

When we got to the restaurant Michael had already gotten us a table. "That's a start." Allie said, "He isn't late."

"Yeah even I'm a little impressed with that." I smiled and we both laughed.

"He's handsome." Brandon said trying to hide his frown. His comment made me giggle. "What? I can appreciate that he is obviously a handsome guy."

"I never told you he wasn't gorgeous." Allie said to him. "I just said I didn't care for him."

"Please." I said, as we got closer to the table. They smiled and nodded at me.

When Michael noticed us coming he stood up, "Hi Love." He said kissing me. "Allie, it's nice to see you again." They awkwardly kissed each other on the cheek, which made me, giggle again. Brandon looked down and smiled at me. "You must be Brandon." Michael said with a big smile. "I have heard a lot about you. I was beginning to think you weren't real." They both chuckled and shook hands.

"Emma does have an over active imagination." He said

"That she does." Michael laughed and kissed my head.

"Oh great, now all three of you can gang up on me." I rolled my eyes and sat down.

"So Brandon, what was it like traveling the world for six years?" Michael asked after we had ordered our food. He seemed genuinely interested in getting to know Brandon and he was being very sweet to

Allie. He had even pulled out her chair for her, which made her look at me funny.

"It was great. I got to see things I had only read about in books. I met some amazing people, and I seriously padded my portfolio." He grinned at me.

"That's why your Dad hired him." I said to Michael.

"Ah." He said smiling. "Yes my father is quite impressed with you. He says the two of you make a good team." I could see him wince slightly and Brandon stop himself from grinning. I really had never seen Michael jealous. "So what made you decide to come back?"

"I decided it was time to grow up. Plus I missed my family." He answered motioning to Allie and me. "Six years is a long time to be away from your best friends." He smiled a smile I knew was meant for me.

"Yeah it is." Allie said with a touch of annoyance in her voice.

"I'm surprise they didn't beat you when you came home." Michael said chuckling.

"It's still early; I've only been home for a couple of days. The magic will wear off. Do you have sisters?" Brandon asked him

"No, I'm an only child." He answered.

"Ah, well they are vicious. And female best friends," he said looking at me, "even worse." He grinned like a little kid.

I giggled, "Yeah once the happiness of you being here wears off, I'm so beating your ass." And we all laughed.

The evening was great. We all got along, joking and laughing. Michael was a sweet as he promised he would be. It made a great first impression on Brandon and threw Allie for a loop with his behavior. When we were about to order dessert Michael looked at his watch.

"Please don't tell me you're leaving." I said frowning.

"I'm sorry love; you know I wouldn't if I didn't need to. The case is almost over and then we can spend all the time you want together." I pouted and he chuckled. "I love you," he whispered in my ear.

"Humph." And crossed my arms across my chest,

"You are seriously like eight years old sometimes." Allie said.

I tried to fight a smile, "fine, fine. Don't work too hard. I will talk to you tomorrow."

Michael laughed, "It's was great to meet you Brandon, and Allie I can honestly say it was a pleasure to see you." he said grinning and leaning over to kiss her cheek then to shake Brandon's hand.

She laughed at his comment. "Right back at ya Michael." She said, "Who knew you could be fun?"

"I surprise even myself sometimes." He said smiling. "Have a great night guys. I love you," he said to me again.

"I love you too, but I'm mad." I said finally losing my fight with my smile.

He laughed again, "frighteningly angry." He said kissing me and then gathering his jacket and leaving.

"Wow!" Allie said when he was gone. "Who was that man and how come he looks so much like Michael?"

"I know right?" I said giggling.

"I hate to say this for obvious reasons, but I like the guy. He definitely loves you." Brandon said with a half smile. "Your slight hesitation did that?"

"Apparently," I answered smiling. "Who knew I had such power. But now that I have this great fiancée, if he slips up I don't know what I'll do."

"Well let's just hope he doesn't slip up then. I don't know if it's possible for him, but I want it to be for your sake."

"Me too," Brandon said

"Me too," I said smiling. "But I really am annoyed he left to go to work." Then I shrugged. "Eh, I won't sweat the small stuff." And we finished our dessert and headed home.

Allie met Brandon and me for lunch the next day. "Do you like, ever work?" Brandon asked her.

"I work hard." She said and smiled. "Do you have any idea what it is like to plan other women's wedding? Chicks are crazy." She laughed.

"Are you planning Emma's wedding?" he asked.

"No." we both said and laughed.

"We agreed a long time ago that she would not plan my wedding. She's my maid of honor I want her to have fun, not worry about whether or not the flowers come on time."

Allie nodded, "Plus it's a conflict of interest when you dislike to groom. Oh sorry," She said quickly when she saw the look on my face. "You know I love you." she grinned.

"You're lucky you're hard to stay mad at. I love you too, Heffa." I laughed and dodged the piece of ice she threw at me from her drink.

"Now girls," Brandon started, "stop fighting." And we both threw ice at him. He laughed and reached out to ruffle both our hair.

"Hey don't mess with the do." Allie said smoothing out her hair. "I have to meet with a crazy bride in an hour. I can't go looking like I just rolled out of bed." Brandon and I looked at each other then reached out and both ruffled her hair. "Ha-ha very funny." She said and took a brush from her bag. "You think you were turning thirteen not thirty." I made a pouty face at her and she smiled triumphantly.

"Don't remind me. Besides you're turning thirty this year too." I pointed out.

"Yeah but you do it first." She grinned. "That party I do get to plan. Oh crap I have to go; I have to be in Cambridge by two." She got up from the table and kissed us both on the cheek. "Love you both, I will call you later."

"Have fun with the crazy bride." Brandon said

"I always do." And she left the restaurant.

"So what are we doing for your birthday?" he asked.

I smiled at him. "It's two months away." I answered him.

"Oh please, I know you well enough to know you have had this planned for ages." He laughed and I smiled at him again.

"We are having a forties theme. And I am getting a jump house."

"You really are eight on the inside aren't you?" I grinned widely. "Who but you gets a jump house for their thirtieth birthday?"

"Um... I can't think of anyone, but I am sure I am not the only one." I shrugged then jumped. "Ooo"

"What?" Brandon said looking at me

"I'm vibrating." I giggled and pulled my phone from my pocket. I looked at it and stuck my tongue out at the phone. "It's Michael."

"Are you going to answer it?"

"If I don't he'll just keep calling."

"He's persistent at least."

I laughed and opened the phone. "Hello."

"Emma?" he said

"No it's Audrey Hepburn, yes of course it's me you called my phone didn't you?"

He chuckled, "Very true. Where are you?"

"I'm having lunch."

"Do you forgive me for leaving last night?"

"I'm thinking about it."

"Tell him no." Brandon whispered and smiled wickedly. I giggled and kicked him gently under the table.

"I really am sorry. I love you."

"I know you are I love you too." Brandon made a face that was somewhere between nauseous and sad at me and turned away.

"Good"

"Hun I am at lunch and it is rude to talk on the phone when you are out with someone. I will talk to you later."

"Are you going back to the office?" he asked

"Yes we are heading there now."

"We?"

"Yes Brandon and I went to lunch with Allie."

"Did they have a good time last night?"

"They did. Allie is still in shock I think."

He chuckled. "Ok well I will call you at the office in a little bit. I love you."

"I love you too, goodbye." And I closed the phone.

"I think I just threw up in my mouth a little bit." Brandon said looking at me with a sick look on his face, then grinning.

"Oh shut up." I said laughing. "Come on, we have to go back.

CHAPTER FOURTEEN

The next month was great. Michael kept his promise to be good. He came over almost every night after work and stayed with me in the morning. He seemed to be handling his jealousy well. He even had dinner with the three of us a few times. Everything was perfect, until about two weeks before my birthday. The party was planned. About forty-five people were coming to have a costume party in my back yard. The bouncy house was ordered and set to arrive the day before. I was getting excited despite the fact that I was rapidly approaching the age of thirty.

What exactly it was in Michael that seemed to snap I am not sure. He had finished his first case soon after he first met Brandon. But about this time he started working on a new case. He started by spending one night a week at the office then two and three. It got to the point where I only saw him on Sunday or if I would spend the night at his house during the week. Sex was basically out of the question. He would be too tired, or when he would want it he would have done something that made me so angry I wouldn't allow him to touch me and I would usually just go home. It had been about two weeks, which was unheard of for us; it had never been a secret that it was what we had the most in common.

I remember the day that things started to go back to the way they were before we got engaged. I had been on the phone with Michael at work. He had called at the last minute because he had a business meeting in the city and had to cancel our plans for the evening. I was upset, but since this was the first time in almost two months he had done it, I decided to let this one go. After all, the man did have to work.

"You're angry." He said to me, I could tell there was actual remorse in his voice.

"No, angry is not the right word. I am upset though; I was really looking forward to this dinner. I love this restaurant."

"I am really sorry babe. Why don't you go anyway? There is no sense of you sitting around just because I have to work."

"It was supposed to be our date night." I said frowning even though he couldn't see it, I was sure he could hear it in my voice.

"I know Love I am sorry. But I promise I will make it up to you."

"You better."

He chuckled, "Do you forgive me?"

"We'll see."

"I love you."

"I love you too." I said and we hung up. "Great." I thought, "Now I have to find someone to go out to eat at the last minute." I knew Allie couldn't come; she had a date, which she was more than excited about. Maybe Brandon was free and could come with me. I picked up the phone.

"What do you want?" He said then chuckled.

"That's very professional." I said trying not to giggle. "What are you doing tonight?"

"Not sure yet," He said, "Why?"

"Michael kind of bailed on me for dinner, and I have reservations at the Inn and I really want to go. So you want to be my date?"

"Oh so I'm back up?" he said trying to sound annoyed, but I could hear the amusement in his voice. "Your man bails on you and you call me like I have no other plans?"

"Do you have other plans?" I asked laughing.

"Not the point."

"I will see you at my house at seven. Look nice." I said and hung up. It would have been a good ending to the conversation if I didn't know what was going to happen next.

"You know," he said opening my door; I sat back in my chair and looked at him amused. "I have a life."

"I know you do."

"I could have big plans."

"I know you could."

"I am in high demand. I'm a catch, I'm cute."

I laughed out loud now. "You are a catch and you are so much more than cute."

"Don't say that." I heard him say under his breath and frown but he recovered quickly. "Then why do you assume I am available?" He was grinning now.

"You are aren't you?"

"Again, not the point."

"Do you want me to take you to dinner at the Inn or not?"

"Oh wait, you're buying?" I rolled my eyes at him and nodded. "Well that changes everything, I'm in." he chuckled. "Can I get prime rib and lobster?"

"You can get filet mignon for all I care; you know I can afford it." I laughed. "I will see you tonight at seven. Now get out of my office, I am a very busy woman." I very rarely talked about how much money I had. I only reason I would joke with he or Allie is because they were both with me when I acquired it. My father had been and investment banker in the 90's during the Clinton era. He had done very well for himself. When my parents died, between the two of them I was left with a little over five million dollars. The only thing I had used the money for was to buy my house; otherwise I had not touched it. I didn't like to think about it really, using the money would only remind me of how I got it. I preferred that it just sit there and I live off the money I made on my own.

"Whoopee!" he said and left my office.

"Dork," I said as he shut the door.

At around six thirty I was still trying to figure out what I was going to wear, when the phone rang.

"Hello love." Michael said.

"Hi Hun, what's up? I am getting ready to go to dinner."

"You found someone to go with?"

"Yes, Brandon and I are going."

"Oh," I could hear the annoyance in his tone.

"Is there a problem?" I said coldly.

"Of course not."

"Good because it's not easy to find someone to go to my favorite restaurant with me when my fiancée backs out at the last possible moment." I said it with a hint of amusement.

"That's true, I'm sorry again. I should be thanking him for going with you."

"Yes you should." I said laughing.

He chuckled lightly, "Ok I will let you go then, have a great night, but don't have too much fun." I just laughed at his statement. "I love you."

"I love you too. I will talk to you tomorrow."

I finished getting dressed right before Brandon showed up. I went to open the door and he was standing there with a big box. "What is that?" I said

"It's part of your birthday present." He said grinning and walking into the house to put the box on the floor.

"My birthday isn't for another two weeks."

136

"I think you better open this one now." he said smiling wider and chuckling.

I looked at him confused. "What is it?"

"Open it." He said. I just looked at him. "Why are you confused? Go open your present. I was driving here and I saw it and I thought, 'Emma needs to have that.' So I bought it and now I am giving it to you."

I smiled at him, "I'm not confused." I said and laughed.

"Sure you aren't. Now open the thing."

I walked over to the box and started to pull off the ribbon, "Why are there holes in the box?" I asked. I was starting to get the feeling of what it was and I was getting so excited I almost bounced when I asked the question.

He chuckled, "Open the box goof ball."

I pulled the ribbon off the box and ripped the top off. Inside was the most adorable bulldog puppy I had ever seen. "Oh Brandon," I said with happy tears in my eyes. "I love him." I walked over and wrapped my arms around him.

He put his arms around me and kissed the top of my head, "I am glad you do. I saw him and I thought you had to have him. You have always wanted a bull dog."

"I have." I said pulling the puppy from the box. "I will call him Bruno. Hi Bruno," I said kissing the dog's muzzle. "We can't go to dinner now." I said looking at Brandon seriously. He laughed. "I'm serious; we can't leave Bruno on his first day in a new place."

"I already called the Inn." He said and reaches around the door to get two bags full of food. "I put it on your tab." He said laughing. "I figured you wouldn't want to leave once you saw this little guy, so I brought the Inn to us."

"That's my Brandon always thinking."

"Yup, always thinking," He grinned down at me.

"Sometimes I think you can read my mind, it's kind of freaky." I smiled at him and lead him into the living room. Brandon had also brought me food for Bruno as well as a bed and some toys. "I can't believe you bought me a puppy for my birthday." I said when we were sitting around watching TV after we had finished eating. Bruno was asleep on my lap and I had my head resting on Brandon's shoulder.

"You wanted a puppy, I saw the puppy, and so I bought the puppy."

"That simple?"

"That simple," He grinned at me. For the first time since he had been home his closeness sent a shock through me. I thought about sitting up straight so I wasn't leaning against him anymore, but somehow I just couldn't. I just stayed where I was trying my best not to react to the electricity running through my blood. Every once in a while he would chuckle, but he wouldn't tell me why.

I was woken up by someone clearing their throat. I opened my eyes to see Michael standing at the end of the couch. "Hi Babe," I said smiling at him. I imagine I had the same smile I had that he loved to see. Because whatever annoyance he felt melted away.

"Hi love." He said and came over to kiss me. I sat up and met his lips.

I looked over at the other side of the couch where Brandon was still sleeping. I could feel my face flush. "I'm sorry about that." I said.

"No worries. You looked comfortable. Plus I've seen you sleeping leaning against his sister too. You're a snuggler," He answered smiling and I giggled. "What's that?" he asked pointing to my lap

"He's my birthday present. Say hello to Bruno."

He made a face at the dog, "That's an ugly dog." He said chuckling.

"So ugly he's the cutest dog ever." I said laughing. Michael chuckled and shook his head. "What are you doing here, I thought you were just going to go home when you finished?"

"I thought about it, but I wanted to see you." I smiled at him, which made him beam at me again. "I really love when that smile is for me." He said leaning down and kissing me again. "I see you never made it to the restaurant." He said motioning to the empty take out bins on the coffee table.

"He brought take out when he brought the puppy."

"Always the thinker that Brandon," He said with a half smile.

"That's what I said." I smiled up at him and he laughed.

"Think you should wake him?"

I turned and looked at Brandon. "Not even a possibility. A tornado could whip through here right now and he wouldn't wake up." I stood up, "Help me." I said to Michael as I tried to pull Brandon so he was lying on the couch. When we had him

settled I looked down at him. He looked very sweet
and handsome when he was asleep. I pulled the
blanket off the back of the couch and put it over
him. "Sweet dreams." I said and kissed my hand
then put it on his forehead,

"Sweet dreams Emma." He said and rolled over. I
smiled and went to meet Michael in the bedroom.

The next morning when I woke up I was alone in
my room. It was a Saturday morning, so I hoped
when I went down stairs Michael would be in the
kitchen. I pulled on a pair of sweat pants and a t-
shirt and went down stairs. I heard someone in the
kitchen but when I turned the corner it was
Brandon. He turned and looked at me with a big
smile on his face. I couldn't help but smile back
even through my disappointment. Then I smiled
even wider when I saw what he was holding.
"Good morning handsome boy." I said to Bruno
who was in Brandon's arms.

"Good morning." Brandon said and smirked. I just
rolled my eyes at him and took the dog from his
arms. "Michael told me to tell you, he is sorry he
had to run, he'll call you tonight, and he loves you a
bunch."

I smiled at him; he was making a face as he said it.
"You look like you're going to be sick." I said
giggling.

"I may, I don't think my body has made up its mind yet." He said and grinned. "I made breakfast." He said and pointed to the table. He had made bacon, eggs, waffles and coffee.

"How did I not smell this?"

"Because you were unconscious to the world," He smiled again.

"Kind of like you last night." I said nudging him.

"Kind of like me every night, who are you kidding?" He laughed. "So I was thinking we could do something today."

"What did you have in mind?" I asked smiling and eating a piece of bacon.

He shrugged and laughed, "I hadn't gotten that far. Not much past breakfast anyway." I laughed at him and started piling food on my plate. "Hungry?" he asked staring at it.

I blushed and smiled, "it smells so good," I laughed. He took a spoon and took half the eggs off of my plate. "Hey!" I said trying to stop him.

"You are not going to eat all these, who do you think you're kidding." He chuckled. I shrugged, he was right I would never finish all the food I took, but I threw a piece of toast at him anyway. "Oh is that what we're going to do then?" he said.

I stuck my tongue out at him. He picked up a waffle and held it up like he was going to throw it at me, "oh bring it on little boy." I said and laughed. He got up from the chair and before I knew it he had flung me over his shoulder. "Hey!" I said giggling. "Put me down."

My whole body was shaking from his laughing which only made me giggle harder. He reached up and tickled my side, I tried to break away and get down but he held me tightly too him. I reach down and started tickling him back. We fell on the floor in a heap with me on top of him. Our faces were so close together I could feel his breath. The longer I stayed where I was the more awkward the moment became, but there was something that was making it impossible to move away from him. He still had that same smell of shaving cream and old spice, it filled my head with familiar memories, and I couldn't help but smile at him. "Emma," he said softly with a smile. "Before you make both of our lives very difficult, please get off of me." He smiled at me like he didn't really want me to move, and much to my own shock, I didn't want to. That same electric current shot through me and I could feel my face start to flush.

"Sorry." I said looking down and feeling slightly embarrassed. I moved so I was sitting beside him now.

He took my chin in his hand. "You have nothing to be sorry for." I smiled at him as Bruno jumped on top of him and started licking his face.

"My little protector," I said laughing. He jumped off Brandon and padded over to sit in my lap. "So what are we doing?" I said smiling at Brandon and scratching Bruno's head.

He shrugged, "I don't know, I was thinking we could take Bruno to the park, and then maybe just rent a movie or something. I miss just hanging out with you. It seems like every time we are together we're at work or someone else is around. I miss my Emma time." He said with a grin then chuckled.

"Aww I miss my Brandon time too." I said and smirked. "But seriously though, I'm starving." I got up from the floor and pulled him to his feet. "Pour me some coffee." I laughed. He rolled his eyes but went to the coffee pot. "Wow! I didn't actually expect you to."

"I needed one too." He said winking and walking back to the table with two mugs in his hands. "Your birthday is getting close. Are you getting excited?" I just looked at him over the brim of my coffee cup and he laughed. "Silly question, Of course you are."

I smiled, "Yeah I think it's going to be a good one. I took the day before the party off. They are going to be coming to deliver the jump house and the tent and someone needs to be here."

"Allie will be here," he pointed out.

"True."

"You know you can't take the day off of work. You know they are going to get you a cake or something."

"That's kind of why I don't want to go." I laughed. "I don't mind being the center of attention when I put myself there, i.e. my party, but I hate when other people put me there, it makes me feel so uncomfortable."

"You're a strange woman." He said chuckling.

"Yeah and I'm your best friend, that has the say something about you." I grinned at him and he rolled his eyes.

"It says I like the company of crazy women," He chuckled.

We spent the rest of the day being sort of lazy. We took Bruno to the park, then to the pet shop so I could buy some supplies, then ran some other errands.

"Why are you buying wood?" he asked me when we stopped at Home Depot.

"I am going to build some stairs." I answered

"Stairs for what?" I turned and looked at him strangely; the thought hadn't occurred to me that he wouldn't know exactly what they were for. But it seemed as soon as I looked at him he did. "You're building stairs so he can get up on to your bed aren't you?" I smiled and nodded. "Lucky dog," He said quietly with a smiled. "You're a goof ball you know that."

"I do in fact know this." I laughed. He helped me build the stairs when we got back to my house. I made us dinner, and then made him do the dishes because of the mess he had left in my kitchen from breakfast. It was a nice quiet evening and he left around ten.

"I should go now; I don't think Michael will like it very much if he finds me here two nights in a row."

"He'll be fine; you were sleeping on the couch. But you're right we shouldn't push it."

"I'll call you tomorrow Emma Grace." He leaned over and kissed the top of my head.

"Ok talk to you then." I wrapped my arms around him and hugged him tightly before he left.

Michael didn't show up that night. The phone rang at about three in the morning.

"Hello?" I answered it sleepily.

"Emma?" the man said

"Yes?" I rubbed my eyes. "Who is this?"

"Emma its Michael."

"Baby why are you calling me at three in the morning? What's the matter? What's going on?"

"Nothing I just missed you and I wanted to hear your voice before I went to bed."

"Are you drunk?" I said with a tired giggle.

"Um…maybe."

"You're drunk." I said, and then got a little annoyed. "Where were you tonight?"

"Me and some of the guys from work went out and had some drinks after we finished up for the night. I guess we lost track of time, I'm sorry did I wake you."

"Yes you woke me." I said laughing again. "Did you have fun?"

"It was ok, I miss you so much Emma, and I wish you were here right now, right beside me, right…"

I interrupted him and giggled, "Yeah I know what you wish. Why don't you get some sleep and come over tomorrow morning and I'll make you breakfast."

"Will you wear your wonder woman panties for me?"

"Yes babe, I will wear them for you."

"Yay!" he chuckled.

"Good night Michael."

"Good night, I love you."

"I love you too."

CHAPTER FIFTEEN

He never made it the next morning; he had to go into the office again. He had to stay late again just about every night that week, same thing for the following weekend, and then most of the next week. He took me to dinner on Wednesday night, three days before my birthday.

"Where is your car?" I asked him when he came to pick me up in an unfamiliar vehicle.

"Um... I had a little fender bender, nothing to serious." He said with a strange smile.

"Are you ok?" I asked him concerned. "What happened?"

He smiled at me with more joy this time, "yes love I'm fine, you should see the other guy" he chuckled. "Just have a bruise on my arm from trying to get out of the car so fast."

"I'm glad you're ok but what happened, did he hit you, you hit him?"

"I was stopped and he came out of nowhere and took out my front bumper." He shrugged.

"Is the other guy ok?"

Michael grinned devilishly, "yeah he's fine, just a few bruises."

I looked at him strangely, "well I am glad you're ok babe."

"Thank you love," He said and we drove to the restaurant.

"I'm sorry I've been working so much." He said to me while we were eating. I looked up at him and just shrugged. I couldn't decide if I was too sad or too angry to say anything else. "Emma, please love, I really am sorry."

"I know you're sorry Michael. You're always sorry." I said and went back to my food. I could see he was starting to get frustrated with me. I just looked up at him. "You promised it would be different. You promised that I wouldn't be sitting home alone at night while you were at work."

"You're hardly sitting home alone." He said coldly.

"I hope you aren't talking about what I think you are. Otherwise this dinner is only going to get more awkward when I get up and walk out." I glared at him for a moment. Over the last couple of weeks he and Brandon had started to have some issues. Neither would ever tell me what it was about. He had also gone back to treating Allie the same as he had before his magical transformation.

150

His face softened. "I'm sorry." He said with a smile. "But you have to admit you spend a lot of time with that boy."

"And his sister."

"But I'm more focused on the boy."

"Maybe I wouldn't have to spend so much time with "that boy" if you ever spent any time with me lately."

"You have a point there." He said and looked down at his plate. "I really am sorry Emma."

"Just please try harder. Go back to being the Michael you were last month."

"I will try Emma I promise. I am just trying to get this case done."

"I can't lose you every time you get a case Michael. I get that it's your job, but work with you always comes first. How am I supposed to start a life with you when I am always second?"

"I know Emma. I promise you are first in my heart."

"I know." I said looking away from him. That was getting a little hard to believe lately.

"I know this isn't the best time for this, but we have a meeting with our lawyers' tomorrow afternoon." He said looking embarrassed. The meeting was about a pre-nup. Michael thought I was against the idea, but the truth was I couldn't be happier about it.

"I'll be there." I said.

"You're taking the whole pre-nup thing very well." He said smiling.

I looked up at him and shrugged. "I think it's a good idea."

"You do?"

"Yes, I'm not marrying you because I think you have money, and you're not marrying me for that reason either." He tried to hide the chuckle that escaped his lips. I glared at him for a moment. The discussion of how much money I had never came up. Michael just assumed I made enough to get by and that was it. He never thought much about my life prior to him being in it. Sometimes I think he believed I hardly lived before I met him. I just rolled my eyes at him, did he think my parents had left me with nothing.

When we got back to my house, Michael went right to bed. He was exhausted from working so much. It had been at least three weeks since we had, had sex and I was starting to get a complex. I took Bruno for a walk, watched some TV then decided to go to bed myself.

When I woke up in the morning he was gone. He didn't leave a note on his pillow this time. I got up and took my shower and got ready for work. When I got down stairs there was a cup of coffee sitting on my kitchen table.

See you at 3

Michael

"Fantastic." I thought and headed to work.

"You're doing what today?" Brandon asked me while he sat at my desk

"What happened to your eye?" I asked suspiciously

He reached up and touched it, "nothing, my face broke up a fight on the T the other night."

"I think you're lying to me." I said looking at him sternly. "What happened Brandon?"

He just smiled at me and I could tell he was trying to come up with something good, "well," he started "I was on the train minding my own business…"

"Why were you on the train?" I interrupted him. I know it seems like a strange thing to be suspicious of, but Brandon hated the train. Anytime he needed to go into Boston he would insist on driving. He would say that the forty bucks for parking was worth not having to squeeze into a sardine can.

He grinned; he knew I was good at this game, "I was coming home from Lansdowne."

"Why were you on Lansdowne?" he also hated clubs.

He chuckled, "I went to Jillian's."

"With who?"

"Why are you giving me the third degree?"

"Because, I want to see how far you're going to go with this lie."

"Why do you assume I'm lying?" he said with a chuckle

"Because I know you better than anyone, now tell me what happened"

He just grinned, "I am trying to tell you what happened, but you keep interrupting me."

I groaned at him, "Fine, fine I am sure you worked on this a long time." I grinned at him.

"What do you think happened?"

"I don't know, but I know you weren't on the T. seriously Brandon when was the last time you took the T?"

"Last night when I went in to Jillian's with Mika and Paul." Ok that was almost believable; he may have taken it if he was going in with his friends from school. "Anyway as I was saying before you rudely interrupted me, I was coming home on the T and was about to get off at the Quincy stop when a fight broke out in front of the door. Some guy threw a punch at another guy and missed, but luckily it connected with my face." He grinned.

"Are you ok?" I asked with a little giggle.

"Of course, I can take a punch." He said smiling, "besides, it wasn't much of a punch it just landed in the right spot."

I reached up and touched his eye, "it looks painful. I'm sorry buddy."

He smiled at me, "no worries, now again, you're doing what today?"

"Way to change the subject Jacobs," I giggled "We're going to the lawyers to draw up a pre-nup."

"That's smart; don't let him get any of your money if something happens."

I laughed, "He doesn't even know I have money."

"He what?" Brandon looked genuinely shocked. "How could you not tell him you have money?"

"It never came up. I think it might deflate his ego a bit if he knew I had more money than him."

"Didn't those great lawyers of his look into what you may have."

I laughed again. "They can't really go looking for something if Michael doesn't tell them too. Plus I think it works out either way. I am going to say that we should each leave with what we came in with and split anything we acquire while married." The truth was I was convinced Michael told them not to look, he liked the idea that I needed to be taken care of.

"Very diplomatic of you."

"Yeah none of this really means anything. I don't exactly plan on divorcing him; I haven't even married him yet."

"Nope not yet," Brandon smiled.

I rolled my eyes at him. "Are you ever going to tell me what happened between the two of you that changed your mind so completely about him?"

He smiled at me, "No I think that is something you need to ask him."

"I have, he gives me the same answer."

"Well then, I think you know the answer to your question then don't you."

I rolled my eyes at him again. "It would really help me out if you told me."

"Emma, I am not making this any harder than it is. I am capable of being civil to him, you love him, and so Allie and I will both just deal."

I pouted, but nodded at him. "Ok I have to head out so I can make it there by three. I will see you tonight."

"You will?" he asked.

"Yeah I am coming over so your sister and I can take care of some last minute stuff for the party. I am taking your advice, I'll be here tomorrow and she has to be there to meet all the vendors."

"Vendors for a birthday party. You are an utterly ridiculous woman you know that." He laughed.

I smiled at him and grabbed my bag. "That's what makes me so lovely." I said. He rolled his eyes at me and I was gone.

I made it to Michael's office a few minutes before three. When I got off the elevator I could see his door open slightly. I walked towards his office and was about to push open the door when my lawyer got off the elevator and called my name.

"Emma." He called out.

I turned around and smiled at him, "Hello George how are you?" when I turned back around Michael's assistant Dawn was coming out of his office. "Hi Dawn." I said to her. She jumped slightly.

"Oh hey Emma, it's nice to see you again." She said and sat down at her desk. She seemed really anxious but I didn't have time to wonder why that was because Michael came out of the office right behind her.

"Hi love." He said kissing me. "George, how are you?" He said extending his hand to shake George's.

"I'm well thank you both, shall we get started?"

"Yes, let me give Phil a call and tell him to head down so we can get this over with. Not the most pleasant part of planning a wedding." He said winking at me.

George chuckled and looked at me. I just smiled back at him. "This should be a cinch, a little shocking to them but an easy deal all around." He whispered to me when Michael had walked into his office.

"I hope so," I said with a half smile.

"It will," He said with a wink and we followed Michael into the room.

When we were all settled around the conference table and Phil had joined us, we got down to business.

"Ok Emma, what would you be looking for if this were to end in divorce? You realize we don't think it will this is simply a precaution."

"Oh I understand that." I said to him. All of Michael's friends thought I was a bit of an airhead mostly because none of them had ever really taken the time to actually have a conversation with me. "I would like the pre-nup to say that we will leave with whatever we came into the marriage with, and we will split whatever we acquire while married."

"Wow really?" Michael said smiling at me.

"Yes of course, why would you think I would want it to be anything else?"

"I don't know, not many women would take that stance on it." Phil said

"I'm not like other women." I pointed out.

"That's very true." Michael said to the other men.

George just smiled, "She is also not looking for any sort of alimony."

"Why are you making this so easy?" Phil asked suspiciously.

"I didn't need any of his money before I met him, what gives me the right to take it after." All of this seemed like a completely normal thing to me, the whole not wanting to be taken care of. Apparently from the suspicious looks I was getting it wasn't normal at all.

"I wouldn't feel right giving you nothing." Michael said smiling

"Ah, you say that now." I laughed. "No truly, I would like it to say that we leave with what we came with and we split what we acquire together."

"You can't change your mind once it's signed." Phil said. He was growing more leery of me with each passing moment. I almost found it amusing.

"Yes Phil, I am aware of that, I am not going to change my mind. Now can we be done with this? Why don't the three of you draw up the paperwork and I will look it over with George and sign it. I have to get to Allie's house there are some last minute details I have to take care of before my birthday this weekend. Will I see you tonight?" I asked turning to Michael.

"No I don't think so; I am trying to get all this work done so I can be with you all weekend." He grinned at me.

I was almost shocked at how unfazed by his words I seemed to be, I was becoming numb again to his absences. "Fine then I will see you tomorrow night." I walked over and kissed him. "Phil, always a pleasure," I said with as little sarcasm as I could muster and shook his hand. "George I will talk to you later, do well for me." I smiled at him and he nodded and kissed my cheek. George had been my lawyer since I was eighteen. He had also been the lawyer for my Dad's firm, and the gentleman I had fought with right after his death. He had been so impressed with my tenacity and how much I reminded him of my Dad that he took me on as a client and we had been working together ever since.

"Have a good night love; I will talk to you later."
Michael called after me. I waved behind me as I
walked out of his office.

"Have a good day Emma." Dawn said as I walked
by. She seemed much calmer now. I wondered if
Michael had been yelling at her before I had come.

"You too Dawn, don't let him work you to hard."

She laughed nervously. "I won't," she said. And I
got into the elevator.

When I got to Allie's she was waiting for me.
Brandon had not come home from work yet. "How
did it go?" she asked when I sat down next to her on
the couch.

"Well I think. George will take good care of me."

"He's a good guy, that George." She laughed,

"That he is." I said and smiled. "So can I ask you
something?"

"What's up?" she said.

"What happened with Michael and Brandon? Why
do they all of a sudden hate each other?"

"Um…" she started ringing her hands. It was
something she did when she had a big secret she

knew she couldn't tell. "I can't tell you." she said and got up from the couch walking towards the kitchen.

"Allison Jacobs you tell me what happened." I said trying to sound as authoritative as I possibly could.

She just laughed at my harsh tone, "Emma I really can't tell you. This is an actual not my place to say could change everything sort of event."

"Allie, if something happened between the two of them, I need to know."

"Then they need to tell you. I'm sorry Emma, this one really is something I can't tell you." as she finished her thought Brandon walked in the door.

"Are you still trying to find out what happened?" he asked me.

"Yes." I said pouting. "And I so thought your sister would be the weak link."

"Hey." She said to me. "There are some secrets I am capable of keeping you know. Not quite as good as the two of you, but I can keep them none the less."

Brandon and I just looked at one another and smiled sheepishly. Some things she didn't need to know. And apparently that is how everyone felt about what happened between the two most important men in my life. No one thought I needed to know, but I knew I did.

"Look all I know is things have gotten weird in my life since it happened, and I want to know why that is."

"Emma please just let it go." Brandon pleaded with me.

"Fine I will let it go for now, but I will find out what happened." I said to him and he just rolled his eyes.

We made the plans for the next day. Allie would spend the day at my house meeting vendors and getting things ready and Brandon and I would meet her there after work before I went to Michael's for dinner.

"So everything is set?" she said to me as I was putting on my coat to leave.

"Yeah I think so. Is there anything we missed?" I asked Brandon.

"Why are you asking me, you two are the party planners? I'm just along for the ride." He grinned at me. His brilliant boyish grin and I blushed.

"Ok then, I think that's everything. Love you both and I will see you tomorrow."

"Night Emm," Allie said and kissed my cheek.

"Night Emma Grace," Brandon said and kissed the top of my head. "I will see you in the morning."

"Good night." I said and I left.

When I got home Bruno met me at the door. "Hello handsome." I said and lifted him into the air to kiss his muzzle. "I missed you today," he licked my face and barked quietly. I put him back down. "You hungry?" he barked again and shook his little butt at me. I laughed and poured him some food, then went to listen to my messages. Then I took Bruno for a walk and got ready for bed.

As I was getting settled the phone rang. "Hello?" I said

"Hi Love." Michael said on the other end. "Did I wake you?"

"No I was just getting ready for bed. What's up?"

"I was wondering if you minded if we had dinner with Ted and Elaine tomorrow night."

"No that's fine sweetie."

"Oh perfect, Elaine will be so excited to see you."

I was so sure she would. All of Michael's friend wives thought I was some sort of freak. None of them were ever excited to see me. "Well I am excited to see her as well." I lied.

"Great, I'm sorry I couldn't be there tonight babe, I love you."

"I love you too. I'll see you tomorrow. Good night." And I hung up the phone. I was a little annoyed that he had changed our date night into a double date, especially with people who didn't care for me much to begin with. I was starting to wonder if I would ever fit in with Michael and his friends.

CHAPTER SIXTEEN

The next day Brandon was in my office again.

"I had a dream about you the other night." I said smirking and looking at him sideways.

He was leaning on my desk and perked up immediately.

"Oh really?" he smiled "Was it a good dream?"

I stopped typing and looked at him like I was trying to remember, I smirked again. "It might have been I can't seem to remember." I giggled and he rolled his eyes,

"You're a tease" he said laughing. I just shrugged and smirked at him again.

Brandon shook his head at me and proceeded to begin to remove himself from my office, when the phone rang. He picked it up. "MacKay Studio's, this is Brandon how can I help you?" he said in his annoyingly chipper phone voice, which always made me giggle. He smiled at me then his face dropped. "Hold please" he said putting the caller on hold. "It's Michael." He said with disgust. Brandon had taken to saying Michael's name like a child says broccoli. I knew he didn't like him, but I guess

I couldn't completely blame him. Michael hadn't exactly been pleasant to be around lately "Oh and remember, as your love just reminded me, always say May I help you not Can."

"Are we going to lunch?" I asked before picking up the phone as he walked out of the room like a hurt puppy.

"If Mr. wonderful doesn't offer to take you first," He snorted. I rolled my eyes at him and picked up the phone.

"Hello, Thank you for calling MacKay studio's this is Emma, how may I help you." I said.

"Hello Love." He cooed into the phone "How is my baby girl doing today?" I hated when he talked to me like I was a child. It was becoming a little too common place and completely out of character for him. I would look at him and say "Michael you do realize that I also went to college and you are only 3 years older than me, please do not speak to me as if I am 12." He would pat me on the head and say "you are sexy when you're angry"

"Hi Hun, what's up?" I asked

"Please do not be angry with me, but I need to work late again tonight. This case is killing me and I have to get it done."

"That's fine I have some work I have to get done anyway."

"Oh thank you baby, will you be at my house when I get home?" he asked. I couldn't tell if he was asking because he didn't want me there, or if he thought he might be horny when he got home.

"Nope I think I am going to stay at my house tonight. I need the dark room Brandon was going to watch Bruno but he likes playing in the back yard." Michael groaned.

"Oh" I could hear the disappointment in his voice. "I was hoping you would be there when I got home, I love to snuggle up to you at night." That made me half smile and half roll my eyes at him.

"I'm sorry sweetie, I really do have a ton of work I need to get done, and I have a deadline you know."

"But I know your boss I can get you an extension." He laughed heartily.

I laughed and told him my mind was made up and I would see him tomorrow. He sighed and said "Ok Love, I will call you later. Tell that boy he needs to learn proper English too wont you love." He always referred to Brandon as that boy lately, as if saying his name would somehow cause him pain. The vague neediness was also new; I really needed to find out what that fight was about.

I laughed, "I will good bye." I hung up relieved for some reason that I did not have to spend another night in Michael condo. I always felt out of place there. The truth was I had already finished my work for the deadline I had Monday, in fact I had finished the work for my next 3 projects, but work was the only excuse Michael would ever accept. As I hung up the phone Brandon was at my door, a huge smirk on his face. "What are you smirking about?" I giggled.

"Mr. wonderful is working late again tonight then?"

"Yes he is."

"So that means you have no plans?"

"I might have big plans you know."

"No you don't Emma I know you too well. So you're free."

"In a manner of speaking. Oh Michael said you should really brush up on your English skills." I laughed,

Brandon groaned. "Did he call me 'that boy' I think it's a nickname I am starting to like." He grinned at me,

"He's jealous of you, you know."

"Me?" Brandon looked at me shocked. "Why would he be jealous of me?"

"Because I spend all my days with you."

"Ah, I see. But he's the one who gets to spend the nights with you." he said looking thoughtful and making the moment slightly intense. "Right ok then I am taking you out for some fun."

"I don't know if I am into your kind of fun." I said with a grin. Knowing that no matter what he had planned I would have fun.

"Oh please." He said. "Everyone loves my kind of fun" he smirked and started to leave the room again. "I am not taking no for an answer, oh and your taking me to Celia's for lunch today."

"Hey it's your turn to buy." I called after him.

He poked his head in the room, "I have to spend all my cash on an English book." And he left.

About an hour later I went to Brandon's office. "Come on butt head let's go." I said sticking my head into his office. "I'm starving and I want some eggplant." He was pretending to ignore me but I could see the smirk on his face. "Hey I'm talking to you." I said moving closer.

"Oh," he pretended to be surprised. "You said butt head and I thought 'surely she can't be talking to me'." He laughed and we were off to lunch.

Near the end of the day and Michael had called about 4 more times. He kept asking me the most ridiculous questions and said he had something extra special he wants to give me tomorrow. I asked for a hint but he said, "It's a surprise," which scared me because the last surprise Michael bought me was a vacuum, I hate cleaning and my house has hardwood floors. Plus I reminded him that my birthday party was the next night. He assured me he remembered and that he wanted everyone to see the surprise. That frightened me even more.

"You ready beautiful?" Brandon said coming into my office. He was wearing a Red Sox hat and t-shirt.

I beamed at him. "Why are you dressed like that?" I asked hoping I already knew the answer.

"Well I told Bob, that his son blew you off again and I was trying to think of something to do for you, so he gave me his tickets." He had the smirk of a child who had just gotten all A's in school.

I jumped up and gave him a hug and a big wet kiss on the cheek. It was only when I heard Bob clear his throat behind Brandon that I realized the hug might have lasted a little too long. We pulled apart and looked at him, both feeling guilty for something as innocent as a hug, or was it.

Bob just laughed and shook his head. He leaned over and kissed my cheek when I thanked him. "Happy birthday dear, I hope you have a wonderful day tomorrow. I wish I could be at your party" He said and placed a box in my hand and left.

"Thank you for everything Bob." I called after him.

Brandon looked at me and chuckled nervously. "What's in the box?" he asked looking at my hand.

I looked down. "I don't know it says not to open until after my birthday." I look at Brandon strangely. "Do you think that is weird?"

"Very." He said "but how is he going to know, he's on vacation until the end of July."

"True, but I won't." and I put the envelope in my bag. "I will put it in my desk at home when I get there, that way I know I won't open it."

We stopped at my house so I could change and we could see Allie. She said everything went really well. She gave her brother an interesting smirk when we told her why we were going to the game instead of me going to Michael's for dinner. He just chuckled and told her to keep quiet. Sometimes their brother sister mental conversations annoyed me and if I didn't love them both so much I might have smacked them every once in a while.

Around five thirty we all left my house. I kissed Allie's cheek good bye. "You kids have fun now," she said winking at her brother.

He just rolled his eyes at her, "I hate you a lot some times," he said.

"But you love me always."

"I hate you both a lot, now let's go. I'll see you tomorrow Al."

"Love ya girl."

"Love ya right back." And Brandon and I were off.

The game was amazing. We played the Yankee's and won, had way too much beer and stuffed our faces full of hot dogs. It was one of the best pre-birthday celebrations I had, had in a long time. After the game was over, and we had sobered up a bit Brandon drove me home. We sat in the car for a while talking and laughing.

He came in and used the bathroom, then played with Bruno for a little while. I watched him, smiling. When he was done I got up to say goodnight to him. He stopped in the doorway.

"Emma?" he asked

"Yeah?" I said looking back at him.

"What time is it?"

"12:25. Why?"

"Oh I just wanted to be the first person to say 'Happy Birthday'" I smiled at him and he beamed back at me.

"Thank you." I said laughing.

"Well you know I like to be number one." He laughed.

I walked back to him in the door. He smiled down at me as a wrapped my arms around his waist. He bent down, kissing my head and hugging me back. "Thank you" I almost whispered.

"For what?" he said. I could have been imagining it but I thought I felt his breath quicken and he held me a little tighter. I stiffened a bit, not because I didn't like him holding me so tight, but because I did. It was bringing back a lot of memories. I still didn't let go; I just looked up at him. He was beaming down at me, which made me giggle. "You smell good." He said absently and then shrugged, "for what?" he said again remembering his question.

"For being you, for being my best friend," I smiled up at him. .

"Well thank you for being my best friend." He said. He smiled at me but it wasn't as brilliant as before. I squeezed him tighter and his smiled got a little bigger. "Ok goofy." He said leaning down to kiss my head. "You get some sleep, big day for you tomorrow old lady."

I pulled back and pouted. "30 is not old. Just because you're a baby doesn't make me old." I said poking his stomach.

He laughed again. "I'm no baby, I'm 27, and I'm a man." He said flexing and then we both laughed. "Ok I'm leaving before I can't," he said. He kissed my head one more time and walked out the door.

My joy for the day I just had confused me. I stood at the window and watched him get into his car and drive away. He must have known I was watching because I could see him laughing as he waved at me one last time. I smiled and shook my head.

Bruno followed me back to my room and climbed up the stairs Brandon and I made him to get on the bed. "What am I going to do buddy?" I asked him he tilted his head to the side and looked at me quizzically. I pat his head. "What do you think could be Michael's big surprise?" A low growl came from Bruno when I said Michaels name. I looked at him, one eyebrow raised. "Michael." I said again and the same growl. I laughed, which seemed to please him. "Hmmm," I looked at him. "Brandon" I said. His head went up and he barked happily. I laughed. "Crazy dog, just like your owner," he seemed pleased that I was done experimenting and settled back down into the bed. I got ready for bed and was asleep almost as soon as my head hit the pillow.

My bed shaking woke me up. I quickly opened my eyes and saw Michael standing over me. "What time is it?" I asked him.

"5am" he answered, a big smile on his face and a bunch of carnations in his hand. "I wanted to be the first to wish you a happy birthday," he said. I smiled up at him; I thought it was better not to tell him that he wasn't. He put the flowers on my nightstand and climbed in beside me and kissed me gently and wrapping his arms around me. "I got you some coffee," he said kissing my neck on one side.

"Uh huh," I breathed.

He looked at my face, quite pleased with himself, of course he knew that he was impossible to resist and I hadn't even started out angry, this time. His bright blue eyes sparkled at me and I gasped to catch my breath. "And I got you some stuffed French toast to eat." He said kissing the other side of my neck.

"Mmm" was all I managed to get out. He laughed into my neck and then kissed me fiercely. I wrapped myself around him, sliding his sweater over his head. He fumbled with his pants. I giggled he smiled and kissed me harder, his reactions, his movements took me by surprise. Today he seemed to be giving me all the things he knew I liked. He took his time, as if he was re-learning how to make love to me. It was every bit as perfect and lovely as it had been in the beginning and I savored each moment not knowing when it would end.

We both fell back onto the bed. He smiled at me triumphantly and I giggled again. "Wow!!" I said rolling over and wrapping my arms around him.

He kissed my head. "Happy birthday baby" he smiled, "I love you."

"I love you too." I said smiling up at him. His liquid blue eyes twinkled with pleasure.

He got up from the bed, causing me to pout. I never knew when I would see this Michael and when he was there I wanted him to stay as long as possible. He looked at my face and laughed. It did not seem like this beautiful version of him would be leaving soon. He kissed my head again, and walked to the bathroom. I still sat on the bed waiting for him to come back. He turned and looked at me again. "I need a shower," he said smiling. I still pouted.

Then he motioned for me to come with one finger and I was up and in his arms in an instant.

We stayed in the shower until there was no more hot water and moved back into the bedroom. At about 8am we decided it was time to get moving. I pulled on my clothes and then stood on the bed to get on his back as he walked me out to the kitchen. When we were on our way down the doorbell rang. I kissed his neck and jumped down walking to the door. I looked back and he winked at me, and then kept walking to the kitchen to put the carnations in water.

I got to the door and opened it to see Brandon and Ally. I smiled wide when I saw them. "Yay!" I said and they laughed and came in. Ally kissed my cheek and Brandon kissed the top of my head. I really was just so much shorter than most of the company I kept.

"Happy Birthday beautiful girl" Ally said handing me a bag.

"Happy birthday lovely" Brandon said handing me a huge bouquet of daisies. I squealed and they both laughed at me again. "So easily amused" he laughed, "I bring you a bunch a weeds and you squeal like a 5 year old."

I pushed him a little and laughed. "Michael is in the kitchen." I saw Brandon make a face at Ally as she rolled her eyes. "Be nice please. He's having a lovely Michael day and I don't feel like kicking him out on my birthday if that changes." They both agreed to be good and we walked back into the kitchen, Ally's arm tightly around my shoulder I imaged it was so Brandon couldn't put his there and make the morning difficult.

Michael smiled at us as we walked into the kitchen. "Good morning Allie" he looked behind us. "Brandon." He said still smiling. "Do you guys want some coffee and breakfast? I figured you would be coming over so I got plenty."

Ally turned and looked at me behind his back "Wow" she mouthed,

"I know right." I mouthed back.

"Lovely" Brandon said poking me from behind. I turned to look at him and he half smiled at me, and then tousled my hair.

"Well Michael," Ally started. "You seem very pleasant this morning." He turned and smiled at her.

I leaned over and whisper loud enough for him to hear in her ear. "It's invasion of the body snatchers." I thought this may have set his mood to bad but he just smiled at me. "Bizarre!" I mouthed to her. She nodded. He really was unfairly beautiful when he smiled like that. It was so rare that I saw this side of him lately that I was always taken aback by it. I just wished that the Michael that was here, the one I loved, didn't make me always forget the other side of him. It made thinking clearly very difficult. He set the food down on the table and laid out 3 plates. I looked up at him confused. "Are you going somewhere?" he looked down at me, the smile still on his face.

"Yes I have some errands to run before the party. Get some last minute work done so I have no distractions." He kissed the top of my head; I thought I saw Brandon cringe out of the corner of my eye and Ally glare at him.

I looked up at him, "What have you done with Michael Mackay?" I asked smiling.

He laughed again, a good sign. "I know I haven't exactly been the best fiancée lately. I am just trying to make up for it a little. Is that ok?" he gave me his best puppy dogface, which made me giggle.

"Lovely Michael" I said.

"Yes love, Lovely Michael." And he laughed. 'Walk me to the door?" he asked.

"Yup" I got up and followed him to the door. He held my hand in his as we walked. "This is nice." I said quietly. "I miss this Michael." I looked up at him, my eyes searching his face for any hint of annoyance. I saw none; all I saw was a bit of pain in his eyes. But I never knew with him, he could be playing games with my head. I hoped he wasn't.

"I am so sorry babe. I haven't been very fair to you lately and I promise things will be different now." his back was to the front door and I was facing him. He seemed to be looking for something in the other room, and he smiled as he picked me up into his arms and kissed me. Fiercely, taking my breath away and making me dizzy.

"Oh" was all I could say and I giggled. I heard a loud noise coming from the kitchen and Michael smirked. I just looked at him confused, hoping he didn't just do what I thought he did.

"Love you baby, I will see you later." He kissed my head again. "See you later Ally. Oh and Brandon," He smirked again and walked out the door. And with him I hoped he hadn't taken my perfect and lovely Michael.

When I went back into the kitchen Brandon and Allie both had forced smiled on their faces. I smiled at both of them. "Ok kids how about we go out into the back yard and check out my circus." They both gave me full grins.

"Can we eat first?" Allie said. "This looks really yummy and I am starving."

I smiled at her, "I think it's cold. Turn on the oven and we can heat it up."

The three of us sat and ate the breakfast that Michael had bought for us. "So what was with him this morning?" Brandon asked. Even without saying his name I could tell he was annoyed about even talking about him.

"I don't know, maybe he feels guilty about being like the old Michael again recently. Or maybe it's my birthday surprise. Who knows?" I was trying not to focus on the fact he had been so awful as of late.

"It's weird and suspicious if you ask me. I wonder if that man gets dizzy from all his mood swings." Allie said

I laughed and shook my head. "I wonder the same thing some times. So what do you say we start getting ready for this party?" I smiled at both of them. Brandon gave me one of his beautiful boyish grins and jumped up.

"I think we should try the jump house out, you know to make sure it ok before everyone else comes over to use it. We don't want anyone getting hurt now do we?" he smirked at me.

"No we certainly don't want that." I jumped up and headed to the back door.

"You two are idiots." Allie said laughing. "Well go on you big dorks, I'll start with the rest of the stuff, I know you won't be any help to me to until you've gone in that thing."

"Thank you dear." I said and kissed her on the cheek taking Brandon's hand and running out the door. "Wait, you don't want to come?"

She smiled at me, "you forget, I was here when they put it up yesterday." And she laughed and turned back to the dishes she was cleaning up. I laughed and turned back to the door.

When we got outside Brandon stopped in his tracks and looked up, "You got a pink princess castle, I can't bounce in a pink princess castle Emm." But he was laughing.

"Sure you can, cause you're my big pink princess man friend." And I laughed as I dragged him the best I could to the opening. I climbed inside "Come on B, come jump with me. Take your shoes off, don't be a wimp. Real men bounce in pink princess castles." I giggled so hard I fell over. He dove through the opening and tackled me as I tried to get up. There was more wrestling going on than jumping.

"So Emma Grace?"

"Yes?"

"How's your birthday so far?"

"So far?" I said turning over on my side to look at him as he lay beside me in the house. "So far, it may be the best birthday I have had in a long time."

"I hope it stays that way."

"Me too." I said and smiled at him. "I think we should probably go and help your sister now. She might come out after us soon."

He chuckled and then helped me to my feet as we crawled out of the opening. We spent the rest of the day getting ready for the party. About twenty minutes before all of the guests showed up, Michael came back. He pretty much avoided Allie and Brandon as much as possible. This surprised me because of how nice he had been to them that morning. It also made me realize that he had been looking to see if Brandon was watching when he kissed me good-bye. I was annoyed with him, but I refused to let him ruin my birthday.

The party was great, and everyone seemed to have a nice time. I of course got way too much food, but luckily I was smart enough to buy enough containers to send people home with it.

"Where did you get this Calzone?" Margo asked me when she was on her sixth piece I think. I only knew because she told me it was.

"I got it from Celia's," I said. "It's delicious isn't it?"

"God yes!! We need to start ordering from there more." She smiled and turned back to her husband.

Almost everyone dressed up. I was dressed like swing girl and Brandon had on a zuit suit. I was kind of glad it wasn't too hot of a day or the poor kid would have passed out. There were military men and nurses and Allie was the piece de resistance. She was dressed like Rosie the Riveter. It was perfect really, she looked just like the poster I had hung on the wall. Everyone seemed to be having a great time. They all loved the food and no one seemed to be getting to drunk because every time we got close we would bounce in the moonwalk and loose the buzz.

There of course was one person who didn't dress up, Michael. He finally came out into the backyard with everyone else when the party was underway. When I looked at him I couldn't help but frown.

"What's the matter love?" he asked me, truly having no idea what could be bothering me. I motioned to what he was wearing and he chuckled. He had on dress pants and a button down shirt. He looked like he had just come from work. "Come on Emma you can't be mad at me for not dressing up."

"Everyone else did Michael," I said pouting. "You couldn't this once step outside yourself and do something goofy for me." I was a little upset, but the truth was I think I would have fallen over if he had actually dressed up.

He chuckled again, "you look beautiful, this look suits you, Classic and classy just like you."

I rolled my eyes at him, "changing the subject?"

He winked at me. "I'm sorry I didn't dress up babe," he said hugging me to him. "But can you still love me knowing that this will never be my thing, but I will always support your goofy side?" he grinned at me. I laughed and nodded. "Good."

"I'm going in the bouncy house, you want to come?" he chuckled and shook his head and I was off to jump in the house with my friends and he sat and watched me. It was so much fun. Eventually I got so tired I laid down in the middle and made people jump around me. I was having the best time and I was getting some pretty good air.

When it got to the present opening I got a little frightened. This is when Michael was going to give me my surprise. Nothing frightened me more than what it could be.

I got a lot of gift cards and picture frames everything was beautiful. I was surprised I got anything at all, I had told people to just come, I didn't need presents, I just needed a party to take my mind off of turning thirty.

Allie gave me a beautiful turtle frame with a picture of her and me on a trip to Hawaii. "I love it thank you." I whispered to her and kissed her cheek.

"Well you wouldn't let me buy you anything big." She said laughing. "You're a pain in the ass by the way." I smiled at her and turned back to my guests. Brandon was about to give me his gift when Michael interrupted him.

"Mine first, if you don't mind?" he said to Brandon.

"Be my guest." He said trying to hide his irritation. I rolled my eyes at Michael and then waited for the big surprise.

He handed me a square box about the size of a paperback book. I looked at him and smiled and then at Allie a bit worried. She shrugged and mouthed, "Its fine." I opened the package and it was a jewelry box from the same place he had gotten my engagement ring. My hand was shaking when I opened the box, not because I was excited about what could be inside, but because I was completely petrified about what I would see when I opened it. Inside was a thick gold chain and hanging from the chain was a gold and ruby carnation. "Oh Michael it's lovely." I said kissing him and trying to do my best not to show on my face how much I wanted to cry. I wondered if this man I loved so much would ever take the time to actually get to know me. I looked at Allie who bit her lip and tried to smile at me. Brandon must have caught my mood because he swooped in.

"Very impressive Michael," He said with a big grin. "That must have cost you a small fortune."

"Nothing is too good for my Emma." He said with a smirk.

Brandon chuckled, "nope, nothing is too good for her." He winked at me and handed me his gift. I smiled half-heartedly at him and took it. "I promise there are no carnations." He whispered in my ear then kissed my cheek.

I giggled and smiled at him, "Thank goodness." I said softly and smiled at Allie who was standing on my other side now.

"You're going to love this." She said with a smirk.

"I hope you didn't spend a lot." I said to him.

"I hardly spent anything, now open it." He grinned his beautiful boyish grin at me.

I pulled off the paper to reveal a leather bound photo album. I looked at him and smiled, tears already stinging my eyes and I hadn't even looked inside yet. "Oh Brandon," I said,

"You haven't even opened it yet." He said chuckling. "You may hate it."

"If this is what I think it is, I could never hate it." I opened the first page and there was a picture of me when I was a baby, my mother holding me, and my father looking down at us adoringly. As I turned the pages there were more and more pictures of my life, the last thirty years all neatly placed page after page. A picture of my parents and me after my first dance recital, pictures of Allie and I when we were kids, picture of my parents and I at my high school graduation, then pictures of me with their family at Christmas and in the summer on vacation. There were more pictures of Brandon and me then I knew was even in existence. It was the greatest present anyone had ever given me.

"Don't cry." Allie said. "If you do, there may be a scene."

I nodded and held my composure. "Thank you Brandon. This is…" but I couldn't find the right words I just smiled at him.

"You're welcome." He said smiling.

"Now that's impressive." Michael said to him with a genuine smile.

"Thank you Michael." He said taken aback by the smile.

"Must have taken you a while to glue all those pictures in there," He chuckled.

I could feel my face flush and my hands balled into fists at my sides. I was becoming shocked at my own anger. Brandon saw the look on my face and smiled then tousled my hair. "Yup," He answered with a grin, "Had to use a lot of glue sticks. Must have taken you a while to pick that necklace out too."

Michael just smirked at him. They seemed to have some sort of mental tug of war going on that they both found amusing. I imaged it had something to do with the fight which annoyed me.

"Ok cake time." Allie said stepping in between them. "It's time for Emma to blow out her candles and make a wish." She glared at the two of them then took my hand. I thought we had been making a scene but it didn't appear anyone had noticed their little testosterone fueled battle and I was grateful for that.

Allie had made me a giant cheesecake for my birthday. Regular cake was not my favorite thing but she knew I loved to blow candles out and I loved cheesecake. When I made my wish, it was simple. I just wished to be happy. No matter what happened I just wanted to be completely happy.

The party thinned out a little later and it was just Michael, Brandon, Allie and me. We all sat around the table on my deck and finished our beers. Michael had pulled me onto his lap and Allie and Brandon sat across from us.

"That was some party." Allie said smiling.

"I had a good time." I said laughing. "I'd say this was one of my top birthdays."

"Well as long as you had a good time, that's all that matters." Michael said kissing me

"Did you not?" I asked him. I could hear Brandon making a noise under his breath across the table.

Michael smiled at me, "no love, I had a good time, I just mean it wouldn't matter because it was all about you."

I smiled back at him. "What do you say we take the jump house for one more ride before they come to get it in the morning?" Brandon said getting up.

"I'm in." Allie said.

I giggled and looked at Michael. "Are you coming?" I asked him.

He laughed at me, "No, grown men shouldn't go in jump houses." He said snickering and looking at Brandon.

"Good thing I'm not old like you then Mike." He said and patted Michael's shoulder as he walked past him. Michael just glared back at him he hated being called Mike.

I went to get up and Michael pulled me back onto his lap. I just looked at him. "Stay here with me." He said, it wasn't so much a question as it was a command

"I want to go in Michael. Its fun, you should try it."

"Emma, jumping in that thing is childish and I would prefer that you not go in it anymore tonight."

"And I would prefer that you did. You can be an old fart if you want to Michael, but I'm not. Remember you said you would always support my goofy side?" I got up from his lap and bounced towards the jump house.

"I'm going to bed." He called after me.

"Ok I'll see you in a bit." And I climbed in and jump around with Allie and Brandon. After about an hour Allie started falling asleep on us, "you should take her home." I said to him.

"You're probably right. I'm glad you had a great birthday Emma."

"Thanks B. I'm so glad you came home and you could be here for it."

"I wouldn't miss it for the world." He said and wrapped his arms around me.

"Thank you." I said and walked him to his car. Each of us now had an arm around Allie.

"I love you guys." She said.

"We love you too." I said and giggled. "I will see you both tomorrow night." I kissed them both on the cheek, waved goodbye as they drove away and went inside.

Michael was sitting up in bed reading a book. "Did you have fun?" He said but it came out cold.

I became defensive immediately, "yes as a matter of fact. You should look in to fun Michael, I think you'd enjoy it."

My anger seemed to amuse him and he chuckled. "I'm glad you had fun love. And I am glad you have people in your life that will bounce in jump houses with you because your fiancée is an old fart."

I laughed at him and got undressed for bed. "You really do need to learn to loosen up." I said.

He smiled at me. "So what's up for tomorrow night?"

"Allie, Brandon and I are going out to dinner. It's sort of tradition."

"Can I come?"

"You want to? You haven't exactly been getting along with them as of late. Are you ever going to tell me what happened?" I asked him with my best innocent face.

He chuckled, "no it's between me and him. Besides it might force you to take a side and I don't want to do that."

"You two are more alike than you think." I pointed out.

"I think what we have in common is our biggest problem." He said and then laughed. "But I really would like to come to dinner with the three of you if you would have me."

"I don't see why not." And I climbed into bed and kissed him goodnight.

CHAPTER SEVENTEEN

The next night the four of us were sitting at a table in the restaurant. It had started at a tradition when I turned nineteen that Allie and Brandon would take me out on our own every year. The conversation started with the three of us reminiscing about my past birthdays. Michael threw in some info here and there about the birthdays he had spent with me, of course leaving out his speech from the year before. He seemed to be genuinely enjoying himself. Then for some reason the topic of conversation came to first kisses. "Jason Jones when I was four" I said.

"No, no." Michael said. "First real kiss."

"Oh" I said laughing. The two martinis' I had already consumed had gone straight to my head and the third I was working on was quickly joining them. "Nick McLaughlin when I was 13" Allie burst out laughter and so did I as both men looked at us confused.

"Nick McLaughlin when I was 13." Allie said and we laughed again. They looked at us like we were crazy. "Oh you don't know he was so tall and goofy and that just made him so cute."

"That's gross." Brandon said now laughing. "I remember that kid." He said looking at me. "He was your first kiss, seriously?" he laughed again.

"Hey he was your sister's too." I said now a little more than drunk. But I think we all were.

"But I thought you had taste, I know she doesn't" Allie tried to kick him under the table and kicked me instead.

"Ouch!"

"Oops!" she said giggling. "Ok Michael who was your first kisses name?"

"Dawn Spencer. I think I was 12." He smiled a little at the memory.

"Aww" Allie and I said at the same time, our giggling now almost out of control. "Wait." I started. "Isn't she your assistant?

He either didn't hear me or he was avoiding the question. "What about you Brandon?" Michael asked not looking at me.

Brandon smirked and Allie laughed louder. "Well?" I said not understanding why they were both so amused.

"Emma." Brandon said.

"What?" I answered which made them laugh harder.

"So goofy, you were my first kiss. I was 15."

"Oh!" I said. I glanced at Michael from the corner of my eye who no longer seemed amused with our reminiscing. But I was too drunk and too curious to stop myself. "Really?" I ask. "That was your first kiss?"

He looked triumphant and Allie punched him in the arm making him deflate only slightly. "Yup" he grinned and winked at me. I thought about it for a minute. If that had been his first kiss, how much better could it get then that? He had practice now. Could it actually be better? But I forced the thoughts out of my head this was not helping anything.

"I would ask you who you all lost your virginity to but I think I might be afraid of the answer." Michael said forcing a smile at me.

Brandon was immediately annoyed. "Mine wouldn't be Emma if that's what you're worried about." He was glaring at Michael.

"I don't need to concern myself with Emma's love life before me. I am more concerned about the one she has right now." He smirked at Brandon wickedly who just glared back at him. "Besides you're a child, she doesn't want a child." I suddenly felt nauseous. I could not believe this was happening. Allie was right; it didn't take long for Michael to do something to make them hate him again.

"You seemed awful concerned for someone who doesn't care." While the two of them argued, all Allie and I could do was look between the two of them like we were watching a tennis match. Michael tried to put his arm around me. I pulled away from him which made Brandon chuckle. "She's not an object, you don't own her." He said

Michael glared at me; the anger was growing on his face. "Don't you even get me involved in this!" I spat at him. "You started it, you asked about first kisses. I didn't even know I was his first kiss. You don't get to put your arm around me for the sole purpose of proving I'm yours. Grow up." I said and stood. Brandon was smirking widely. "Don't." I said to him. "Don't you make this any worse, I'm not mad at you yet, don't change that." He bit his lip to stop him grin. I just rolled my eyes at him.

"Emma, sit down." Michael said angrily. I turned and glared at him again.

"Don't tell me what to do. Why couldn't you be good, why couldn't you be the lovely Michael tonight. Just one night I wanted you to not start trouble. One night where you were nice to the people *I* love. I'm nice to your friends all the time.

These people are my family Michael. You knew this was our thing, you wanted to come, why do you have to be such an ass sometimes." There were tears streaming down my cheeks now, which seemed to infuriate Allie.

"Come on Emma." She said and took my hand leading me out the restaurant.

"Where are you going?" Michael asked glaring at the two of us and then moving to stand in front of Brandon who was following.

"Are you going to fight me?" Brandon asked somewhat amused. "Because that's really going to help your cause big guy. You have her; she's going to be your wife. I'm just a guy she kissed twelve years ago who gets to be her best friend now. Listen to your girlfriend buddy grow up. You need to realize how lucky you are that she picked you and act like you know it, or you're going to lose her. Now get out of my way before I have to do something that upsets her more than you already have." Michael looked defeated and then moved out of the way.

"I'm sorry." He said.

I started to walk towards him and then stopped myself. I thought I would let him fester in his grief for a while. I was getting tired of letting him off the hook so easily when he flashed his baby blue eyes at me. I was still furious and I wasn't going to let him charm his way out of it this time. Instead I just turned and walked out of the door.

"I'm sorry." Brandon said when the three of us where outside.

"Why are you sorry?" I asked him and Allie smiled at me. She had been afraid I would take Michael's side, I could tell by the look on her face. "Did you really think I would take his side in that situation? You know me better than that."

She laughed, "Suddenly you seem to have a much clearer head about things than you have had lately." She grinned at her brother who rolled his eyes at her.

"I haven't the slightest idea what you are talking about." I said. "And you have no reason to be sorry, you didn't do anything wrong. I am the one who should be sorry."

"Why are you sorry? You shouldn't have to apologize for what he does." He said looking at me with a serious look on his face.

"I brought him. I should have left him at home."

He put his arm around me. "We were going to be around him sooner or later, and I am pretty sure the outcome wouldn't have been much different on another night." I frowned at his words, mainly because I knew he was probably right. "I don't hate him entirely. I can't really blame him for being jealous; I would be too if the roles were reversed. But I don't like him. I don't like the way he tries to treat you like a possession." He frowned down at me.

"That annoyed you too?" I said and laughed. He shook his head not laughing. "I know." I said finally and looked down.

"Emma." I heard from behind me. When I turned to look at him Brandon still had his arm around me. I could see from the look on his face he was not happy about what he saw. This immediately made me defensive. "Can I talk to you please?" he asked

I walked over to him and Brandon and Allie wandered slightly to give us privacy. "What do you want?" I asked.

He blinked at me, his beautiful blue eyes full of something I didn't recognize. I finally decided it was fear. "I'm so sorry I reacted like that. I know they are your family and I was horrible. It was my fault; I did bring up the first kiss. I was just taken aback by his answer is all. I'm not use to being jealous, or feeling threatened in anyway. This is all new to me, but I trust you completely and I am so sorry. I promise I will be better." He looked at me and my resolve was starting to fail. He looked over my shoulder. "I am sorry to both of you as well. My behavior was uncalled for. I am sorry I ruined your night out together. You both mean the world to Emma and she means the world to me."

"I've heard that before. Do you think you can actually do it this time?" I said.

"We can look past it if Emma really wants us to," Brandon said narrowing his eyes.

Michaels face became slightly annoyed then relaxed. "That sound like a fair trade." He said. "Can I take you home?"

"No I don't think so." I answered. "He may be able to look past it, but I need a little more time. Why don't you go home and I will call you tomorrow." His face could not hide his annoyance. "Don't mess with me right now Michael. I'm drunk and annoyed and not in the mood for your attitude."

"Are you always this confrontational when you're drunk? I don't think I have ever seen you like this."

"Yeah I bring my back bone when I drink vodka. Now go home."

"I'm sorry again." He said to Allie and Brandon as he walked towards his car.

"Ok well this has been a fun night. We didn't even get to eat." Allie said.

"Ah that's why I'm so drunk." I said laughing. "Let's go back to my house, we'll order in Chinese food and watch sixteen candles." I smiled at Brandon.

"I'm in for the Chinese, but if we are going to watch an eighties movie can it at least be the 'Breakfast Club'?"

I laughed, "Oh, ok." I said and the three of us walked to my house. The rest of the night we talked and ate and watched movies we hardly talked about the incident with Michael. They both promised me that they would try to forget it happened. I didn't entirely believe them, but I wanted to.

It was fun. I almost forgot how much I loved being with both of them, even when they ganged up on me. It felt like the last couple of months I hadn't had this time with them. I was happy and for the first time in a long time I felt I was complete. I felt like I was home.

CHAPTER EIGHTEEN

The next day at work I was paying for the night before. I walked by Margo into my office with a grunt. She laughed. "Did we drink a little too much last night?" she said. I just looked at her and she laughed again. "There is a present for you on your desk." She said and went back to typing.

When I walked into my office there was an enormous bouquet of carnation. "Gah!" I said and I heard Margo giggle again.

"Carnations are sheik." She said

"Carnations are hideous." I said and closed the door. I thought about tossing them into the garbage but I moved them to the window and opened the card.

Emma,

I am so sorry baby.

I'll make it up to you, I promise

I love you

Love,

Michael.

"He made an effort." I heard from the doorway. I turned and saw Brandon standing there with a smile. "He may have made a poor effort, but it's at least an effort."

I smiled back at him. "How can someone I love so much, know me so little."

"He is clearly not a favorite flower knowing kind of guy."

I laughed, "Yeah maybe. It doesn't really seem like his style does it?"

"Not from what I can tell." He grinned and came into the office and sat at my desk.

"Are you here to make me feel better again, or do you have another purpose?"

"I always want to make you feel better, but I am here on a work related quest. We have to do that shoot in the park today."

"Oh I totally forgot about that."

He chuckled, "from what I heard you worked for six weeks to land this shoot."

I laughed, "Oh I did, but my mind is a bit scattered as of late. I haven't really felt like myself. But it's starting to get better." I said and smiled at him. "I'm still so glad your home Brandon. I feel like everything is almost perfect now."

"Almost?"

"Yeah I can't quite put my finger on what's missing yet. But I am sure I will figure it out."

"I hope you do." He grinned. "You ready?"

"I was born ready." I said and giggled. He rolled his eyes at me and we left the office.

"Have a good day kids." Margo said laughing as we walked by her desk. "Don't do anything I wouldn't do." She said. I shot her a look over my shoulder and she laughed harder.

The shoot was for a summer camp. There were kids running everywhere. We had brought a bunch of camp props and just let them play while we took candid's. About an hour into it Brandon decided he wanted to get in on the fun and grabbed a potato sack and started racing with the kids. I couldn't take the pictures fast enough. They all loved him. The girls looked at him all googly eyed and you could tell the boys just wanted to be him.

The owner of the camp came over to stand next to me while I was taking the shots.

"Remind me that if I ever have anything else I need photo's taken for, or if I need entertainment for my kid's birthday party I should call the two of you."

I laughed and smiled at him. I showed him a few of the shots on the camera and he seemed more than pleased. "I'll get the thumb nails ready for you tonight so you can pick the ones for the pamphlet."

"I knew you would be the best Emma." He said.

"I aim to please John." When I finally wrangled Brandon we met Allie for lunch again in the park.

"How ya doing kid?" she asked me with a smile.

"I'm fine, still paying a bit for drinking so much, but I had fun. I feel like it's been months since the three of us had a movie night. I wish it was for different circumstances though."

"We all do." Brandon said with a half smile.

"Oh. I'm vibrating." I said pulling my phone from my pocket.

"It's like he knows when you're at lunch with us." Brandon said slightly annoyed.

"He's psychic like that." I said to him. "Hello?"

"Are you still mad at me?" he said before even saying hello.

"Yes." I answered him. I knew he had asked the question first because he had assumed I had gotten over it.

"Are you going to forgive me?" he asked.

"I can't talk to you about this right now. I am having lunch with Allie and Brandon."

"Are you discussing how awful I am?" He said amused, which annoyed me.

"No you didn't come up in conversation at all actually." I said coldly.

He chuckled softly. "Can I come over tonight so we can talk about it?"

"Tonight? Yeah I guess that would be fine. But I am hanging up now."

"Ok love I will call you at work in a little while."

"Fine," I looked at Allie and Brandon and they were whispering something to each other.

"I love you," he said

"I love you too." I said, but as I did I felt a little sick. What was happening to the perfect life I had all set up for myself?

"You're going to let him come back so soon?" Allie asked. She wasn't annoyed, but I could tell she wasn't happy with my decision.

"He's coming over so we can talk, that's all."

"He needs to do more than talk, he needs to grovel."
She said.

I rolled my eyes, "I know he does, I am going to
attempt to understand why he did it. I don't know
what else to do here. I may be mad, and he may be a
jerk, but it doesn't change the fact that I love him."

"Gah!" she said and looked at Brandon. "Are you
not going to chime in here and help me?"

He just looked at her, "I want you to do whatever
makes you happy Emma." He said to me, no trace
of a smile on his face. "If you think taking him back
will make you happy, then I am for it."

"Coward," Allie whispered to him.

"What am I suppose to do Allison?" he almost spat
at her. He must have been more frustrated with the
situation then he was letting on, because he never
called his sister by her full name.

"You know." She said looking at him, then turned
and looked at me. "I want you to be happy too. And
I hope you are going to realize what that is soon,
because you're driving me crazy." But she was
smiling slightly.

"I don't want to talk about this anymore." I said.

"That's fine." She said. "I have to go anyway. I am going to call you tonight to see how things went. Please for the love of god; think about when you're the happiest. I love you too much to see you having so much sadness." She kissed me on the cheek and tousled her brother's hair then left.

"What makes me the happiest?" I said to him.

He smiled and shrugged, "I can't tell you that Emma, and you need to figure it out for yourself. Come on we have to get back to the office." And we left.

When we got back to the office we got the thumbnails together of the shoot so we could pick the best one to show the customer for the layout. When we finished we were leaving the conference room.

"Emma, Michael is on line one." Margo called out to me when we stepped out of the office.

Brandon groaned, "I'll see you later." He said and walked off to his office

"Thank you Margo." I said as I walked past her into my own office. "Good afternoon Mackay Studio's this is Emma how may I help you?" I said into the phone, always with the proper phone etiquette.

"Hello love." He said

"Hi Michael, what's up?"

"I'm just calling to say hi. I was wondering…" oh this was always bad. He was going to change plans on me, or cancel all together.

"What were you wondering?" I said distracted.

"Well, would you mind if you came to my house tonight. Ted and Elaine wanted to have dinner and I thought that…"

"You thought that even though I am angry with you that I would come to your house and cook dinner for your friends and pretend that you didn't make me look like a complete ass last night?"

"Emma don't you think your being a bit mellow dramatic."

"Michael don't you think you're being a complete prick?" the anger I was feeling was almost overwhelming, but at the same time I felt great, I felt like myself again. For the first time in almost two years I felt like I deserved to be treated better. I heard a faint giggle coming from outside my office. I knew Margo could hear my end of the conversation and I knew she would get a kick out of it. She tried to be supportive like everyone else, but she didn't care for Michael much either, at least not when it came to me.

"Excuse me?" he said angrily. "I think that…"

"I don't care what you think right now Michael. You know what I think, I think that you should make your own dinner for your friends and you should explain to them the reason that your fiancée isn't there to serve them their wine and cheese is because you made a fool of her in front of her two best friends and are now instead of making it up to her like you promised, you want her to be some sort of servant to you when you should be kissing her feet and making her feel like you actually care." I took a deep breath.

"What's going on with you Emma? You never act like this."

"Maybe I'm just tired of all the I'm sorry's that you never seem to mean, or the way you make me feel like I am not as smart as you because I didn't go to Harvard like all your friends did. If you want to be my husband you need to make me feel like you want to be."

"You know that I love you."

"Do I?" I said coldly. "Look this is not the place for this and I am starting to draw a crowd" I said as I looked up and saw Brandon and Margo in the doorway, I was sure she went to get him when she heard me fighting with Michael. Maybe it wasn't the whole world out to get me; maybe it was just my office.

"So you're not coming over tonight?"

"Have you heard nothing I've said Michael?"

"I'll tell them not to come over; it will just be you and I."

"You're not even sorry at all are you?"

"I am. Why would you say that? I sent you flowers didn't I?"

I laughed loudly, "Oh yes you did, p.s. Michael I HATE carnations." And I hung up on him. "Well that was fun." I said and looked at Brandon and Margo in the doorway. Margo looked guilty but Brandon looked like a combination between worried and furious. I took a deep breath and smiled at him. "It will be fine, don't look so upset ok."

"Emma." He said looking at me seriously.

"Really B, I'll be fine. I think I am just going to call it a day." I said getting up from my desk. "I will call you later ok?" I said to him as I grabbed my bag from my closet. "Call John and tell him we have the thumb nails. You can take them to him or we can go see him on Monday to finalize everything."

As I went to walk by him he grabbed me and wrapped his arms around me. "I'm so sorry this is happening to you Emma."

"Thank you." I said looking up at him, trying my hardest to stop the tears from streaming down my face. I pulled myself away and left the office as Margo touched my hand as I walk by.

"You'll figure it out, I know you will." She said.

I just looked at her, I had no idea what it was I would figure out that everyone else was so convinced would come to me. It only confused me more, which didn't help my already unstable emotional state. When I pulled up to my house, there was someone sitting on my front porch. I pulled into the driveway and got out. He stood up and walked towards me.

"Emma." He said.

"Michael." I said back and started to walk past him. "What are you doing here?"

"I called the office after you hung up on me and they told me you went home."

"I'm having kind of a bad day." I said coldly and attempted to un-lock my front door.

"I'm sorry Emma." He said

"You're always sorry Michael." I answered not looking at him. "I just can't understand how someone I love so much can know me so little. It's infuriating."

"Emma, please." He pleaded and I heard his voice crack. It was the first time I had looked at his face since getting out of the car.

"Are you crying?" I asked him. I was trying not to sound disgusted when I asked. I wasn't, but I was afraid my tone would come out as if I were.

"I don't want to lose you," he said. "Please don't tell me I already have."

"Michael, I…"

"Please Emma, will you come over tonight, I'll make *you* dinner and we can talk. Please Emm, I can't lose you, not like this. Not for something so stupid." I just glared at him and he sighed. "I mean something so stupid that I did. I just need you to forgive me."

"When did this become so complicated?" I asked him.

"I don't really want to answer that, but I am not ready to give up without fighting."

"I don't know." I looked up at him and I was starting to cry. "I don't think I can take anymore. Your mood swings make me dizzy and I don't think my heart has any more space to keep breaking."

"Just come over and talk, that's all I'm asking."

"Fine, I will be there at seven. I need to go lay down for a bit. I won't be able to talk at all if I don't rest a little."

"Seven is perfect. I love you Emma."

"I love you too Michael."

"I hope that's enough for you to forgive me."

I stopped and looked up at him, "so do I." I said and walked through the front door closing it behind me. Bruno met me at the door and I picked him up and walked over to the couch. It wasn't just this one incident that made me so angry with Michael; it was a combination of things, of moments. Sometimes he made me feel like he kept me around just until something better came along. But the truth was I did love him. Things weren't always bad there were good moments. If nothing else I would at least give him the opportunity to talk, to explain his behavior and hopefully he would show me why it is I should stay with him.

I fell asleep on the couch for a bit. I was woken up by at knock at the front door. It took me a minute to realize what it was and Bruno and I groggily went to open it. Bruno started barking happily at the door before I could get it open. I smiled at him. When I opened the door Brandon was standing there with a concerned look on his face.

"Hey you," I said smiling.

"Hey, how are you doing?"

"I'll live." I answered. "What's up?"

"I came to check on you. You looked really bad when you left today and I wanted to make sure you were ok." He forced a smile.

"I've had better days." I said moving out of the way so he could come in. "what time is it? I think I've been out cold for a while."

"It's about five thirty." He said coming in and sitting down on the couch with Bruno in his lap.

"Ok good." I said and sat beside him.

"Are you going somewhere?" he asked curious.

"I'm going to Michael's. He was here when I got home and I told him I would come over so we could talk and figure some stuff out."

Brandon looked angry when I said this. "What could he possibly say?" he said coldly.

"I don't know that's why I am going." I said trying not to sound aggravated.

"You think he deserves that? You think he deserves you?"

"I don't know Brandon." I said now unable to hide the agitation I was feeling. "I can't just throw away two years of my life without at least hearing him out."

"So you're going to go back to him even though he clearly doesn't know you at all. Even though he treats you like a trophy instead of his fiancée. Even though he isn't remotely good enough for you?"

"Did I say I was going back to him?" I said coldly. "Did I say I don't hate how he treats me some times, how he doesn't seem to know any of the small stuff about me and how he can't seem to get along with the people I love? And really Brandon is anyone ever going to be good enough. At least he makes the effort. At least he tells me how he feels. I didn't have to spend years trying to guess, he's never disappeared on me either. It may not always be good but at least he's here."

Brandon looked down at me shocked. The truth is I was shocked too. I never realized just how angry I had been with him for leaving all those years until that moment. He looked like I had just punched him in the stomach. "Emma I had no idea I…"

"It doesn't matter now does it?" I said unable to stop the words from coming out so coldly. "What is your problem? Spit it out; just say what you want to say." I was expecting him to yell back. I was expecting him to tell me that Michael just wasn't the one and I should keep looking. I expected him to stick to his guns. What I didn't expect was the reaction I got.

"I'm sorry Emma." He said, and when he said it I knew he wasn't just talking about what he had said to me in the last ten minutes. "I don't think I can ever explain to you how sorry I am." He said and got up. I looked up at him; I could feel the tears sliding down my cheeks. "It wasn't supposed to be like this you know. I don't know what is was supposed to be like, but it wasn't this." I nodded up at him. "You're my best friend Emma Grace, nothing or no one will ever change that." He pulled me up from the couch and wrapped his arms around me. "I only want you to be with someone who knows what he has and won't for a second take that for granted."

"Brandon…"

He put his hand over my mouth, "its ok. We're ok, I promise. I just have crap timing" he smiled. "I'm going to go now. Go to Michael's, hear him out. Either way I know you will make the right decision for yourself."

I wrapped my arms around his neck tightly. "I have no idea what I'm doing."

He chuckled a little. "When has that ever stopped you?" He looked at my face and smiled. "I will call you later. Why don't you take tomorrow off too? I think you need a little break." I nodded again. "I will talk to you later Emm."

All I could do was nod again. I wanted to say something. To say something that would make the pain in his eyes go away, but I couldn't think of anything. So I just kissed him on the cheek and let him go.

When I got to Michael's about an hour later he had dinner waiting for me. The lights were dimmed and he had put candles on the table. I was a little annoyed. He was going to try to use his charm to get himself out of trouble again, so when he went into the kitchen to bring out the food, I turned up the lights and blew out the candles.

"Yeah I didn't really think you would appreciate the romantic ambiance." He said with a nervous laugh. "Just a force of habit I guess." I just smiled at him and sat down. "So are you going to talk?" he asked.

"No, you are. You see if I say too much, I am going to say something you won't care for, and I have had enough fighting with men for one day."

He looked at me curiously. "You care to elaborate on the plural?"

"Nope," I said and put some food on my plate.

He shook his head trying to get rid of his annoyance with my answer. "Ok. I have no excuses for the way that I acted the other night. The way I have been acting for the last few weeks." I nodded. "I don't know why I do what I do. I have no idea why I thought you liked carnations. It's come to my attention that I haven't paid much attention to the little things about you for a long time. And I know I don't deserve it, but I love you Emma, more than I have ever loved anyone, and I just want to have an opportunity to maybe try and get to know you again."

"I don't know if I have it in me anymore Michael."

"Give me a week, just a week to prove to you I know what I would be losing."

"You think you can fix this in a week."

"No, but I think I can prove to you it's important to me to fix it."

"I'll give you till Friday."

"I'll take it." He said and jumped up from his seat to come over and swing me around.

I couldn't help it, I giggled a little, "put me down please, I just finished eating and this could end badly." He put me down and I half smiled at him. "Thank you for dinner, but I think I am going to go now. I've had a long day."

"Ok love, I will see you tomorrow."

"Ok good night."

"I love you Emma." He said kissing me.

I looked up at him, "I love you too." I said. No matter how much I wished I didn't sometimes, it was inescapable. I was in love with him.

CHAPTER NINETEEN

I took the next day off and Michael spent most of the day with me. The rest of the week I barely spoke to Brandon at work. He was frustrated that I was giving Michael another chance. He promised he would get over it but he was annoyed with Michael not with me. "I get that you love him Emma, but you need to understand it is going to take us more than a few days to get over this." He said us because Allie was also frustrated with me. Except she made it clear it was me she was annoyed with.

"You're irritating." She said to me when I called her on Friday afternoon.

"I know," Was all I could say.

"Although I am proud of you for yelling at my brother."

"I didn't yell." I said.

"Either way, whatever you said, he needed to hear." She laughed. "What are you doing tonight?"

"I am going to Michael's. We are supposed to be having a nice quiet evening so I can decide if he has made the right amount of effort."

"And has he?"

"Not sure yet. I'm so confused and I have no idea why."

"Because you're and idiot," She said.

"Oh Allie you always know just what to say to make me feel better." I laughed.

"I know what are best friends for? Ok doll, love you bunches, call me later."

"I will. I'll give you all the gory details."

"That's my girl. Later."

"Later." I said and hung up.

When I got to Michael's that night he was on the phone. I sat in my chair, the only one I liked in his condo and read my book and he paced back and forth in the kitchen whispering to someone and becoming obviously irritated, I should probably have listened to what he was saying but I couldn't be bothered. I shook my head at him and went back to reading.

"Who was that?" I ask him as he walked back into the room.

"Um... No one" he said seeming slightly nervous "What are you reading?" he asked kissing the top of my head.

226

"Nothing you would be interested in" I smirked up at him.

"Ah smut," he laughed. He took his paper and sat down on the couch.

"Actually it's a photography book. The pictures are amazing." I turned to face him and spun the book around so he could see the picture I was looking at. "I mean look at this picture; you can see every blade of grass. Doesn't it make you want to be there?"

He made a face at me. "It's just a picture Emma." He said turning back to his paper.

"I knew you wouldn't get it," I said laughing.

He smiled and then stopped. "Emm I was thinking, maybe we should start looking to move in together now. I mean if we are going to be married it just makes good sense."

I thought for a moment "it does?" I said almost as a question and then I realized what he meant. "You mean economically" I said.

"Yes of course" he said. I rolled my eyes but he didn't catch it. "So maybe we should look into selling your...."

"We should what?" I interrupted him

"Your house Emma, We should look into selling it"

"No"

"Emma, be reasonable."

"I am being reasonable. I am not selling my house to move into this glorified apartment. There is no yard, no animals allowed and no room for kids. No absolutely not." I was furious and was now standing over him.

"Emma it makes more sense to live here?"

"What sense does it make Michael? What sense does giving up my dream house to live in a place with a doorman make?"

I could see from his face that he was getting angry and annoyed. But I didn't care. I was fed up with this relationship and he wasn't use to me fighting back. After two years I thought I had lost my intensity. "What am I suppose to do with Bruno?"

"Give him back to the boy" I heard him say under his breath.

"What???? Seriously Michael this is how you end the week you are supposed to be proving how much you love me?"

"Come on Emma your making a huge deal out of nothing. It's just a house."

"And this is just a condo, why can't you sell this place."

"I don't want to" he stood up, his 6'2 frame towering about my 5'4 one. "When you are my wife, you will do what I ask of you. We are going to sell your house and live here, we are getting rid of that ugly dog, we will have children when I am ready, you will quit your job and stay home and take care of my house and lastly you will stop hanging around that boy and his sister" he was staring down at me. Something that I had seen him do to a lot to men, men who always back down, so Michael was not prepared for what came next.

I punched him, as hard as I could I punch him in the face sending him falling back onto the couch. I stood above him staring down. "You listen here Mackay; I have had enough of your crap. I am not selling my house, I love it and it's mine. I will have children when I damn well please you are not in charge of my body. I love my job and I will not give it up for you or anyone because YOU are not in charge of my life. The dog stays because he was a gift and I love him enormously. And lastly, 'the boy' and Allie, are my best friends. They know me better than anyone, including you. You will not tell me what to do, you will not run my life and" I looked down at my finger "you will not be my husband" I took the ring off and dropped it on the table. I grabbed my purse and I left leaving Michael sitting there open mouthed.

I felt ill. "What have I just done" I thought to myself as I stepped into the parking garage. "And why hasn't he come after me?" I was starting to get annoyed again when he came flying out of the stairwell.

"Emma wait" he yelled out of breath. He ran over to me and placed his hand on my shoulder to steady himself. I was tempted to push it away and watch him fall, but I didn't. "I am so sorry; I can't tell you how sorry I am. I don't know why I said those things I am just stressed out about work and…" he stopped and stared at my face. "Of course we will sell the condo and not your house. And I know how much you love your job I would never ask you to quit, and Bruno is cute in his own little way and 'the boy', I mean Brandon; I will just have to learn to accept it. After all I trust you completely. So please take this back, and say you will be my wife." He slipped the ring back onto my finger and I just stared at it, and then him.

"Michael, I…."

"Please Emma; I love you so much, please forgive me."

"I will think about it." I said, half smiling at him. "Just give me the weekend to think. I will call you Monday."

"Ok, ok I will take that. I really am so sorry Emma; I didn't mean any of it."

"Ok." Was all I could say? Then I got in my car and drove away leaving him standing in the parking garage watching me go.

I drove for what seemed like hours. The ring sat on the dashboard, staring at me, mocking me.

"What am I doing?" I asked myself. I turned the car around and drove back to Michael's. When I got to his door I took a deep breath and walked in. what I saw when I did I was not prepared for. Michael's assistant Dawn was walking out of his bedroom naked. I gasped.

"Oh, oh Emma," She said.

Michael flew out of the bedroom and looked at me. "Emma, sweet heart this isn't what it looks like."

I stared at him for a moment. "Do you think I am a complete moron? I mean granted things are just starting to make sense, but really Michael it's not what it looks like? Was she taking a letter for you naked?"

"Emma." Dawn started.

I turned and looked at her, "how long has this been going on?" I asked her.

"About five months." She said and looked down ashamed.

"You should be ashamed." I told her.

"You've been with Brandon this whole time." Michael spat at me.

I looked at him sideways. "I've been with Brandon so much because you're never around and apparently it's because you've screwing your secretary. I never touched Brandon like that. Not once. It's not like that with him and I, and you know it. I have been faithful to you our whole relationship."

He looked at me, "not once."

"Not once, not even a kiss. I told you, Brandon and I are just friends"

"Emma, I…"

"Oh save it." I said. "If you thought I was cheating on you, the right thing to do is not to cheat on me you idiot." I turned and looked at Dawn. "I would really appreciate it if you put some clothes on please." She looked down at herself and then hurried into the bedroom. "None of this even matters. It makes me want to throw up, but it doesn't change anything anyway."

"What do you mean it doesn't matter?" he asked.

"I came back because I had an epiphany in the car."

"Oh and what was that?" he said snickering.

"That you don't love me." the look on his face was a cross between shock and anger. "You don't love me, and no matter how much I love you it doesn't change that."

"How can you say I don't love you?" he said coldly.

"If you loved me, you would know me better. Two years is long enough for you to know my favorite flower. It's long enough for you to know I would never cheat on you and if you loved me you wouldn't be sleeping with Dawn."

"I told you why I was sleeping with her." Dawn came out of the bedroom and looked at him. I looked at her face and smiled.

"Don't do to her what you did to me Michael. I think she might be in love with you." I walked over to where they were standing. "Be careful and know you will never be first. I don't really blame you after all. I mean look at him, he's completely magnificent looking." I said to Dawn. "He's not all bad, just mostly."

"I'm sorry." She said.

"I wish I could tell you its ok, but it's not. I don't think you're a bad person for it, but I do think you're a whore." She looked like she wanted to say something but stopped. "And you." I said turning to Michael. "I believe this belongs to you." I took the ring from my pocket and handed it to him. "I hated this you know. You did everything wrong. But I told myself it didn't matter. Not the ring, not the place, not the way you asked me just that you asked. I don't know when I lost myself when I was with you, but I will get me back."

"You'll fall on your ass without me."

I turned and looked at him, "I've got padding back there, I'll bounce right back up." I heard a quiet giggle from Dawn and I left the condo. Before I could get back to my car I started crying. I picked up the phone. "Allie."

"Emma honey what's the matter, what happened what did he do what's wrong?"

"Please come and get me, I don't think I can drive. Ask Brandon to come so he can take my car home too please"

234

"I'm on my way." And she hung up. I walked over to my car and got in. I put my head on the steering wheel and sobbed. I felt stupid, how could I not see what was happening. How could I have been so wrong about someone I loved so much? Before I knew it my car door was being opened and I was being pulled out of the car.

"Hi." He said a concerned smile on his face.

"Hi." I said back.

"Allie is going to drive you; I'll take your car home ok?"

"Don't you ever get tired of rescuing me?" I asked him with a smile.

"Emma Grace, I will never get tired of rescuing you." He said and kissed my head as he helped me into his sister's car.

She was sitting behind the wheel of the car looking at me. I half smiled at her and she pounced on me, wrapping her arms around my shoulders. "Did you break up?" I nodded. "Why?"

"You want to original reason or the thing that solidified it?"

"Give me the original reason first."

"He doesn't love me Allie. The only person Michael Mackay loves is himself. He didn't make me happy anymore, really I don't know if he ever did."

She reached across the seat and squeezed my hand. "And the thing that solidified your decision?"

"He's fucking his secretary."

She slammed on the breaks. "He's what?"

"Yup, we had a fight tonight so I left and drove around for a bit. Then it sort of came to me that all we do is fight and that is no way to spend my life, so I went back to talk to him and when I opened the door she came walking out of the bedroom naked."

"Did you punch her?"

"No, it's kind of pathetic really; I think she's in love with him."

"Did you punch him?"

"Not for this."

"But you punched him?"

"Yeah during the first fight, I've had a hell of a week." I said with a half smile.

"Oh woman," She said. "What are we going to do?"

"Well tomorrow we are calling a lock smith."

"Um…why?"

"Because I forgot to get my damn key back," I said with a small laugh.

"You have a bazaar way of looking at things, have I ever told you that?"

"Yup," I said. Suddenly my phone started ringing. I looked at it.

"Who is it?"

"Who else?" I said. "What?" I answered it.

"Are you going to come back here so we can talk about this?"

"Are you kidding me?"

"Emma, you're being ridiculous, you know I love you. Dawn means nothing to me."

"Wow Michael, just when I though you couldn't be any more of a prick you go and surprise me. I will be by tomorrow night to get my things. I will drop yours off while I am there, including your key."

"So you're just giving up then?" he asked

"Why shouldn't I? It's hard to be in a relationship when the other person isn't there. And in case you forgot, you fucked your secretary ass hole." And I hung up on him.

"I'm proud of you." She said as we pulled into my driveway.

"I kind of am too, But that doesn't stop me from wanting to eat like a whole cheesecake."

She stopped the car and leaned over to kiss my head, "We'll get you through this." She said with a smile. I nodded and got out of the car.

"I don't know what I would do without the two of you. You know that right?"

"Yup," She said and laughed as she linked her arm in mine and we walked to my front door.

When the three of us were inside Brandon let Bruno out into the back yard and the two of them sat on either side of me. "What happened?" he asked.

I looked at Allie, "How's your temper today little brother?"

"Depends on the answer to my question," He said looking at her strangely.

I shook my head at her. "Then you get the short version." I said.

"That seems a little unfair," he said looking at me.

I put my hand on his cheek and smiled, "You flipping out will only make this harder, I will tell you the whole story tomorrow. Ok?"

"Ok." He said accepting defeat. "So what's the short version?"

"Basically I realized that Michael didn't really love me."

"I think he did. I know he did, he's just a selfish prick. He can't really help that."

"Are you defending him? Maybe I should give you the whole story." I said

He chuckled and put his arm around me. "I'm definitely not defending him. I can't stand him and maybe someday I'll tell you all about the fight we had. But I promise that he loved you. He just didn't deserve you."

"He didn't make me happy."

"Which is why he didn't deserve you," Allie pointed out.

"I love you both, you know that?"

Allie looked at her brother and smiled. "Yeah, we know."

"Will you guys stay here tonight? I don't think he'll come by, but just in case I would really like to not be alone in the house."

"Of course," Brandon said with a grin and Allie giggled.

"We'll stay as long as you need us Emm, it's not like you don't have the space for us." I smiled at her and got up. "Where are you going?"

"I need food and wine and I am letting my dog back in the house." The rest of the night I managed to only cry in little spurts.

CHAPTER TWENTY

By the time the morning came I was crying more because I felt stupid than anything else. I was so mad for having wasted so much time. The locksmith came and changed all the locks. I gave Allie and Brandon the new keys.

"I'll be back in a bit ok." Brandon said kissing the top of my head,

"Where are you going?" I asked suspiciously thinking he had the idea to go kick Michael's ass.

He laughed and tousled my hair. "I just have some errands to run. Don't go to Michael's without me ok."

"I won't." I said. "I have some errands to run as well. Take your sister home, she has a wedding today."

"I will see you in a couple of hours." He said

"I will be back after the wedding." Allie said kissing my cheek. "I was going to ask you if you wanted to meet Craig tonight too." Brandon gave her a dirty look and I giggled.

"Oh I would love to. I need to meet this Guy." I said looking at Brandon. "He's the first guy your sister has been interested in a long time."

"Yay!" she exclaimed. "Ok I will call you later."

As they were walking out the door it heard Brandon say to her, "Really AL you're going to flaunt your happiness in front of her tonight."

"I need a little happiness." I called after him. "Plus she knows me well enough that if it bothered me I would say no." Allie turned and stuck her tongue out at him. He shook his head at both of us.

"You women are crazy." He said and the two of them were gone.

When I was alone again I got dressed and headed out to run some errands and do some grocery shopping. While I was driving around Michael kept calling my phone. I eventually put it on silent and finished what I was doing. When I was on my way back to my house I checked the phone. I have 20 missed calls and about 14 messages. I pulled over into the park and listened to them.

"Emma its Michael, baby I am sorry again, please…" I deleted it

"Emma, please come ba….." deleted

There were 9 more like this one. Then the last three messages changed everything.

"Emma, it's Michael, something happened please call my cell."

"Emma, its Brandon, please call me, something happened"

And the last "Emma, its Sophia, honey please call one of us, Bob had a heart attack. We are at Mass General, please come."

Before I could finish dialing her number I was back on 93N and 5 minutes from the hospital. Brandon answered her phone.

"Emma?"

"Brandon?"

"Hi sweaty, are you on your way?"

"I am. I am almost there. How is he?

"Not sure yet. I'm not family so they won't tell me anything. Basically I am the stuff holder while Sophie and Michael run around. Just get here ok."

"Yup I am pulling in the parking lot now. Miracles happen I hit no traffic."

I parked my car and ran to the waiting room.
Brandon was waiting at the elevator and I hugged
him and whispered "thank you" although I don't
think he heard me.

He walked me into the waiting room where Sophie
was sitting and Michael was in the corner she rolled
her eye in his direction when she saw me. I smiled,
and leaned down to give her a kiss.

"How is he?"

"He's in surgery now" she said as I sat beside her
and took her hand. She kissed it and said "thank you
for being here." I smiled at her. Brandon sat on her
other side and held her hand. She kissed his as
well. "You two are amazing. A gift from God" she
smiled sadly and we sat there, the three of us
together while Michael yelled at someone on the
phone across the room. I was sure it wasn't about
his father.

About an hour later Brandon and I were in the
cafeteria getting coffee for everyone. "Ok" I
started, "this may sound so bad, but I think you
know me well enough to know I don't mean it the
way that it sounds but that I mean it in…"

"Yes, yes babbles. I am here because Sophie called
me to find you and when none of us could find you
I knew you would come right here when you heard

so I came here so I could be here for you.' He smiled his adorable boyish grin.

"That's creepy."

He looked shocked. "That I came?"

"No, that you knew exactly what I was going to ask before it came out of my mouth. Creepy" I giggled. "But I am so grateful you are here." And I hugged him. His body tightened slightly, and then relaxed as he kissed the top of my head.

"I'd do anything for you Emma Grace. Besides you know I love Bob too."

"I know but thank you."

"Are you going to tell Sophie about you and Michael?"

"Not yet. I think I am going to wait until we know that Bob is going to be ok. I don't want her to have to think about that now."

"You're a good person Emma."

"Right back at you B," I said and took his hand as the two of us walked back to the waiting room.

CHAPTER TWENTY-ONE

I tiptoed into Bob's room making sure not to wake him if he had drifted to sleep. Sophie had told me he wanted to talk to me. I walked in and peaked around the curtain.

"Hey Kido!" he said excitedly and then winced slightly but the smile never faded.

"Hey Bob. How are you doing? Do you need anything?" I asked inching closer.

"I am going to be just fine dear. Now sit. I need to speak to you."

I pulled a chair over to the bed and sat. He took my left hand in his and got a strange look on his face. He pulled my hand towards his face and looked at me quizzically, but I saw a hint of what I thought was hopefulness in his eyes. He was staring at my lack of engagement ring. I blushed. "I must have left it at home." I answered the question I could see forming. I didn't want to upset him any more when he was in this state. I thought telling him about Michael and I could wait for another time.

"Uh huh" he said smiling. "I'm sure you did. Where is my son anyway?"

I slight feeling or anger shot through my body and I could feel my face become flush. "When you got out of surgery he went back to the office" I said, almost unable to hide the disgust I felt.

Bob simple chuckled. I looked at him slightly alarmed. "That doesn't surprise me. Honestly Emma I don't know where he comes from. He is my only child, but he is a stranger." he looked sad now. I understood exactly what he was saying. "Did you open your present yet?" he asked becoming chipper again.

"Oh no my present" I thought immediately. He must have been able to read my face because he chuckled again. "You would forget your head if it wasn't attached" he said smiling. I blushed and smiled. "Anyway, I wanted to talk to you about some things. You know that I love you like a daughter, right?"

"Of course," I said. And it was true. In the eight years I had known Bob he had treated me like I was his family, even before I started dating Michael. But this question now, here made me nervous.

"Good, good." He said. He pulled my hand back up to his face and kissed it. "This," he stared showing me my own hand naked, ring less. "This makes me happy." I looked at him unable to hide my confusion. "There is nothing I would love more than for you to be an official member of my family, but…" he stopped for a moment. I thought he was trying to gage for response to what he was saying. I had no other emotion but confusion. "My son is no good for you." he said looking almost ashamed at his words. "When I first met you, you were full of tenacity and life, when you started dating Michael I saw you lose some of that."

"When you met me I was 22, all 22 you olds are tenacious." I pointed out.

He chuckled again but continued. "This is true, but you were different. For the first six years I knew you, no matter where you were, no matter who was there, you were full of life, happy. Then when you started dating Michael, it seemed that you started to lose it. You were almost being lost in his shadow, when you use to be the one shining the light. But, six months ago I watched it slowly come back, your life, your happiness and the only time I don't see it is when you are standing in my son's shadow."

I could feel the tears streaming down my face, involuntary, soaking my cheeks. "Bob…" I started.

"Emma please let me finish." He said almost scolding but the warmth was still in his eyes and he smiled slightly. "Six months ago something happened that changed everything." He said looking at my face for some kind of recognition to what he was saying. There was none. He sighed and squeezed my hand. "Think about what I said, think about what could have happened that changed you. I know you will see it, Sophie knows it too. She's not as gung hoe about the idea, but she wants our son to be happy too. Go home and open your present. Come see me tomorrow and let me know what you think." He smiled. "I know you will love it." He had a smug little smirk on his face now that made me giggle a bit. He put his hand to my cheek. "Happiness," Was all he said and smiled. "I am tired now, could you please send Sophie back in. she is the person I have looked at before going to bed for the last 35 years. I can't change that now." He smiled. I smiled back, kissed his hand and nodded.

When I left his room, Sophie was standing outside the door already. She looked at my face and smiled. She wrapped her arms around me and then pulled me back to look at my face again. "I have loved that man since the moment I laid eyes on him when I was 16 years old. Not a day goes by that I don't know he's the one, I never question it. When you don't know in your very core that it's right, then it isn't. It isn't always easy, but it should never be so hard you want to give up, or you lose yourself. You know I love my son, and I can't say I am totally happy but from what he tells me you made the right choice. I will tell Bob if you would like?"

"I didn't want to upset him." I said with the tears still streaming down my face.

"Please don't think him a bad father Emma. You and Michael are not right for each other. It will make him happy to know you figured that out. And when you figure out what it was that changed it all, he will be even happier. Now go." She kissed my forehead and walked into his room.

I noticed she made a point to say that he would be happy. My head was spinning as I walked back into the lobby. More tears fell from my eyes and I could feel it coming, I started to fall but someone caught me. "Emma?" I recognized the voice, so sweet and melodic. "Emma?" this voice was different, more harsh and commanding. It made me jump and open my eyes as I saw them both standing there. Brandon had been the one to catch me. He looked at me, concern on his face, fear in his eyes. Michael was standing over me glaring down at me. He looked nothing more than annoyed, no concern or feeling in his eyes. I got up with Brandon's help and glared up at him. Brandon looked at the two of us and said "um... Yeah I'll be over there."

The longer I glared at him the more his face softened. "You..." I growled at him. He took a step backwards.

"Emma, calm down." He said with still a hint of annoyance in his voice.

"I'm leaving." I said turning away from him.

"I'm coming with you" he said as if I did not have a choice.

I spun back around and glared at him again. "NO YOU WON'T" I growled again. "You will stay here and see your father or go back to the office or whatever it is you feel like doing. I am going home, and you're not coming. You're not my fiancée anymore Michael. You don't get any more claims on me." He reached out to touch me and I pushed his hand away. I could see the anger coming back to his face as he clenched his hands into fists. Brandon saw it too and came running over.

"Ok time to go." He said pushing me towards the elevator, my pocketbook in his hand. "Here" he said to Michael giving him Sophie's purse. "Do something useful and give this to your Mom." And he walked fast to catch up with me. We rode in the elevator silently. More tears escaped my eyes. "I'm going to drive you home; when you feel better you can drive me back to get my car, ok?"

It was an actually question, not a command. I simply nodded knowing I couldn't drive myself. We drove to my house, again in silence. We got to the house and went inside. It had started to pour. I was soaked He helped me take my jacket off and hung his up as well. I looked up at him. He looked back at me with concern in his eyes he put his hand on my cheek. "What did Bob say to you?" he asked in almost a whisper. That is when I lost it. I started to sob, deep painful weeping sobs. My body began to shake. Before I knew it he had me in his arms and was walking over to the couch. I cried into his shoulder tears soaking his shirt, but he didn't let go. He simply held me close to him, rocking back and forth and repeating, "Its ok, its ok."

I woke up still in Brandon's arms. He was asleep now as well, peaceful and handsome. I slid from his arms and walked to my desk where Bob's gift waited. There was a note on the desk when I got there.

Emma,

When I walked in I saw you and my brother tangled up on the couch

I thought it best not to wake you

But woman you are so going to explain that to me.

I will call you tomorrow.

Love you, Allie

I laughed at her note; I could only imagine what she thought. I sat down and slowly opened the envelope that Bob had given me. Inside were a letter and another envelope. I read the letter.

Dearest Emma,

We hope you had a lovely birthday; we apologize for not attending the event. We would like to start with the bad first. It is always good to start with the bad and work back to the good.

I could tell immediately by this line that Bob had been the one to write the actual note. I smiled to myself and kept reading.

The bad news is that I have decided to retire.

I have been doing this for so long and my Sophie wants to travel.

I paused, my heart leaping into my throat. How could he make these words good in anyway. But I continued.

I know that is does not seem that any good can come of this from your eyes, but I have chosen a more than perfect person to give the company to.

I.... I mean we have chosen you Emma. You have been like the daughter we never had since the moment you came into our lives. And we believe you will make the company thrive as only you can.

I know this seems like a lot to take in, but I promise, I, I mean we know you are more than capable

When you have certain people by your side. We will be waiting for your answer.

Love, Bob and Sophie.

p.s. when it comes to our son please think about what you are doing. Sometimes things we need and things that will make us far happier are right in front of us.

We just need to open our eyes wide enough to see them

I stared at the note; in the other envelope were papers for the company. Each paper outlined my takeover. It was all too much for me to handle and I began to sob again, trying, without success to be quiet enough that I would not wake Brandon on the couch. Before I knew it he was beside me. Fear in his eyes.

"Emma" he whispered. He pushed the hair from my face and stared at me "please tell me what's going on."

CHAPTER TWENTY-TWO

I started to speak and looked into his eyes. I gasped, in that moment I understood what Bob had said to me, who he was talking about. I understood what everyone had been talking about. I understood it, finally, because I hadn't looked at him through these eyes in a long time, eyes that weren't clouded by my loyalty to someone else. I grabbed his face and kissed him. Lightly at first, but then something seemed to click in his brain he pulled away and looked at me, differently now, euphoric and hungry is the best way I can describe it. "Emma?" he breathed my name like it was the question and the answer at the same time. In an instant I was in his arms. His lips back on mine, fiercely now, pulling me towards him. I wrapped my arms around his neck, pulling him closer to me. His hands were tangled in my hair, his tongue tracing my lips and circling my tongue. Our breath quickened as he walked us over to the couch. He sat down with me on top of him, sliding his hands up my sides and back to my face. I groan came from my lips that was almost animal like. It made us both giggle. And then he stopped.

"No" I whispered kissing his ear.

He laughed and made his own noise, kissing me again quickly and then pulling away again. "Emma" he said again, I giggled like I have never heard him speak my name before and I kissed his neck. He laughed again and pushed me away. "You're making this hard woman, stop." I made a pouting face at him. He shook his head at me, still laughing. "Do you have any idea what you are doing?" he was more serious now and the weight of his question hit me. I just looked at him shocked but I knew he could tell I understood the question. "Well?" he asked again.

"I know exactly what I am doing" I said placing my hand on his cheek. He still looked at me seriously even though the joy was evident in his eyes. "I am just going about it all wrong." I said shaking my head and getting up. "I didn't see.... I didn't expect...." I motioned to him and he was on his feet and had me in his arms in an instant, I looked up at him. "Tonight, Bob told me that I lost myself when I was with Michael." He made a face and winced at the name. I reached up and stroked his cheek again. "But then he said something happened six months ago. Something that made me... well me again. And I just didn't understand. And then you sister was saying things and everyone else and then this letter and well I..." I looked down. "I didn't know. I didn't see. But when I looked at you tonight it was like I was looking at you with brand new eyes. Seeing all the things I should have seen six months ago when you came back. The things I was too afraid to see." I stopped speaking and looked up at him. He had a smile on his face that was half smug and half expectant. He raised one eye brown as if to say "well?" and I giggled. "Brandon Jacobs you are the reason I smile every day at work, the reason I smile at all." I looked up at him through my eyelashes, and smiled.

"Emma you are killing me, please, please just say it." His face looked tortured even though he still smiled down at me.

"Wait" I said looking at him. Pulling away and running to the door. His expression was half confused and half annoyed. "When I tell you this, when I finally say it out loud, I want there to be nothing in the way, nothing to worry about when I say it, just you and me. There is something I need to do." He understood immediately.

"You have to do that now?" he asked

I just looked at him. "I want him out of my life completely. I don't want any part of him left when I finally say what I should have said years ago."

"Do you want me to come with you?" He asked, hoping I would say yes. I think the gloating alone would make him explode.

"Do you want to?" I asked, already knowing the answer. He smiled and bounded towards the door. "But if he is there please be good."

"I will grab his box of stuff." He said picking it up and carrying it out the door. He kissed the top of my head. "Emma, I will be very good, I will not make this harder for you than it already is." He looked into my eyes. "Are you sure, are you sure this is what you really want?"

"I have never been surer of anything in my life." I smiled at him and we were out the door. I called Sophie at the hospital; she told me Michael had gone back to the office again. I asked her if she needed anything while we were out.

"No love." She said. "Come and see us tomorrow and we will talk about your present"

"Oh Sophie about that…"

"No, no love, you go do what you need to do. Tomorrow is another day, I think you are dealing with the most you can for today. Tomorrow is another day" and then she hung up.

I hung up the phone and turned to look at Brandon while he was driving. "What?" he said looking a bit worried.

"What I weird Fucking day," Was all I could say? He laughed and took my hand. He kissed it and kept driving. "He's at the office"

"Of course he is" he said and drove the rest of the way occasionally squeezing my hand. When we pulled up to Michael's building I looked at him and took a deep breath. "Ready" he asked.

"As I will ever be" I turned and smiled at him. We walked up to the elevator and took it to Michael's floor. The fact that Michael wasn't home only made this trip slightly easier. It wasn't that I was upset about removing him from my life; I was just still so annoyed with myself for taking so long to figure things out.

"Do you want me to come in with you?" he asked kissing the top of my head.

"I think I do. He isn't in there anyway. If you come it will go quicker."

He nodded and walked with me through the door when I unlocked it. I took a deep breath before opening the door. It swung open in my hand and I gasped. Brandon was at my side in a second. Michael and Dawn were on the couch. I laughed a little. "Still not use to that." I said. Brandon looked down at me. Brandon started to walk across the room, for what I assumed was to knock Michael on his ass. I stopped him. I smiled spread wide across my face. "Don't worry this is only slightly worse than the scene I saw yesterday." I said to him.

He looked at me with shock, "This is what the two of you wouldn't tell me?"

"Yes, and now I see it was a good decision." I said and held his hand tightly so he wouldn't leave my side.

"What are you doing here Emma?" Michael asked annoyed. "Have you finally come to your senses?"

"I told you I would be coming to get my things. Your mother told me you were at the office so I figured now was a good time. And seriously, I caught you actually having sex with her this time. Gross by the way."

"Why is he here?" he asked motioning to Brandon.

I smiled widely up at Brandon and giggled. "He came to help me get rid of you from my life." I took the box from him and put it on the floor. "Everything is in there, including most of the gifts you gave me. If you don't mind I am just going to get my things and then I will be out of your life."

"Wait let me understand this, you're leaving me."

I turned and looked at him as I gathered up the few things I had left in his condo. "Are you kidding me right now?" I asked him laughing. "I think you may be mentally unstable." I said to him. "I left you Friday when I caught you with her." I said motioning towards Dawn, who had wrapped herself in the blanket on the couch. She was beginning to look annoyed. "I realized something today though. And I just want to be rid of you." I turned and looked at Dawn, "You should really get out now."

Michael laughed. "You and the boy, oh that's rich. And what can he give you Emma. Everything you have in this world you have because of me. You are nothing without me. Useless, you'll be back." Before I realized what had happened Michael was flying into the wall. Brandon had hit him before he could finish talking.

"You arrogant fuck." He almost spat the words out. "You have done nothing for her. Everything she has is hers. You had nothing to do with it. I have spent the last six months listening to you belittle her and treat her like she was a piece of property instead of the woman you are suppose to love. You don't deserve her, you never did" he grabbed my hand and pulled me to the door. A shocked look on Michael and Dawn's face and a look are pure joy on mine.

When we were in the elevator he put his head against the wall and took a few deep breathes. He still had my hand as a gazed up at him. He opened one eye and looked down at me. I beamed up at him

261

and he smirked. I wanted to jump into his arms and kiss him but I stopped myself. I could tell that now was not the time.

"Maybe you should drive me to get my car." He said. I felt like someone had put a pin in me to deflate me.

"Ok." I said unable to hide the sadness in my voice.

He picked up my chin with his hand and look into my face, "you still have something very important you have to tell me. I just need to drive around and clear my head for a while. I will come back" I nodded again and headed back to the hospital and stopped at his car. He took my face in his hands again and kissed me. I was glad I had put the car in part. He pulled me almost into the passenger seat the way he smelt the way he tasted made me dizzy, how could I not have noticed this before. He pulled away from me and I slumped back into the driver's side. "I won't be long I promise. I just need to calm down."

"Brandon I…" he interrupted me

"No, not yet. Please just wait till I get there. I want to savor the words when you finally say them"

I smiled at him. "Hurry" I whispered in his ear letting my lips brush against it. I felt him shake and almost growl which made me giggle and he jumped out of the car while he had the chance.

I drove back to my house and realized almost instantly why Brandon really took off. Sitting on my porch was Michael. I should have known but I think I was hoping for a different outcome. When he saw me pulling in he stood up with his hands out as if to say 'please stay calm.' I got out but I think I was unable to stay calm. "You changed the locks" he said annoyed, "Where is the boy?" he couldn't stop himself from asking, "Emma please listen love." The word made me glare at him.

I took a deep breath and walked over to him. "Michael let's be honest, even if you hadn't been screwing your secretary for the last 5 months I was coming over to end this the other day anyway. We don't really love each other. I can't be myself around you; I don't like myself around you. And quite frankly you're an ass hole and I don't want to be around you if at all possible, you pretty much make me feel sick."

I could see the anger growing in him again. "And I suppose you love him then. That boy?"

I just smiled at him. "That is really none of your business. If it makes you feel better we can just say that the reason we aren't together any more is because you are screwing your secretary and call it the end. Either way it's the end. I don't even know if I can truly be mad at you for much longer. I am just too damn happy for that. You made this easier on me. But it doesn't make it ok and it doesn't make me hate you any less. Now leave."

"Emma!"

"Leave!!" I growled at him spinning to glare. He turned and walked to his car.

"If I leave" he started. "I won't come back. This is over. Think about that."

"It already is over, now leave!" I repeated. And he did. I sat down on the porch for a second to gather my thoughts. "What a fucking day." I said to myself again shaking my head. I jumped up and ran into the house. Suddenly giddy. Bruno met me at the door. "Hey buddy, mommy has to get dressed." He was excited and followed me into my room. I brushed my hair and put on a cute dress and went back to sit on the couch. Suddenly the weight of the day hit me and I could barely keep my eyes open. I tried to fight it but soon I was fast asleep.

I woke up suddenly when it felt like I was floating. I realized that I was being carried into the bedroom. I look up and he smiled at me. "You got all dressed up for me." He said grinning. I could only manage a nod. "You look beautiful, but you always look beautiful." And he kissed my fore head. The shot of heat his lips sent through my body suddenly woke me up.

"Put me down." I almost yelled. He looked at my face confused. "Please Brandon put me down" he did as I asked and took a step back hurt in his eyes. I smiled at him and took a step forward to re close the space between us. He seemed to relax when I did it. "This can't wait till morning. I have waited years to realize this and now I want to shout it. So please just sit."

He smiled at me smugly. "Oh." He said, "Are we having a talk" he chuckled and sat in the closest dining room chair.

I rolled my eyes at him and started. "I should have realized the first time you smiled at me that it was so much more than I ever thought possible. You, Brandon Jacobs, are the reason I have any spark left. You make me laugh harder than anyone, you always know what I am thinking before I even speak, you make every day of my life worth…" he didn't let me finish speaking I was in his arms again kissing me fiercely. I started to wrap myself around him then pushed away again laughing. "Can you please control yourself until I finish." He grumbled at me but smirked and sat back down. I took a deep breath. "Where was I… oh yes, you make every day of my life worth living and I love you more than any woman has ever loved a man."

He was tapping his foot impatiently. "Are you finished?" he asked smugly.

"Um…Yes I think I am" I smirked back at him and walked towards him. He picked me up and spun me around, then sat me on the chair. "Um… Hello I am waiting on some kissing here." I said slightly annoyed. He held one hand up to me and grinned. "Two seconds ago you couldn't even wait for me to say I love you." I giggled when I heard myself say it. "So why am I all of a sudden being tortured." I pouted.

He shook his head at me and laughed. "Excuse me Miss 'I just figured out 3 hours ago I can't live without you' I have about 12 years of torture under my belt you can wait a few minutes for me to get some stuff off my chest." I sat in the chair crossing my arms and pouting. He raised an eyebrow at me and fought a smile at the corners of his mouth. He attempts at being serious were becoming weak. He came and kneeled down in front of me. I was still attempting to pout, but the twinkle in his dark eyes made me shiver and I smiled. He smiled at me triumphantly, and then kissed my forehead. I just shook my head. "Ok shhh my turn woman." I stuck my tongue out at him and he laughed. "I have loved you since the first time I saw you. You were sitting in the lunchroom with Allie. You had on the cute little black dress you always wore for special occasions. It was the first day of my freshman year and you were the most beautiful girl I had ever laid eyes on."

"That wasn't the first time you saw me." I corrected feeling a little victorious at my memory. He immediately shot me down.

He rolled his eyes at me. "No it wasn't the first time I met you but it was the first time I SAW you. When you became something other than Ally's best friend. Now stop interrupting Me.," he said feigning an angry face, which made me giggle. He laughed to and then stroked my cheek. I pushed my cheek against his hand. His touch sent a shock through my whole body and I had to sit on my hands to not attack him. This made him laugh harder. "Oh hell, I love you too." He said and pulled me up into his arms. The taste of his tongue in my mouth made me want him more. I wrapped my hands in his hair pulling him into me. He stumbled towards the bedroom, I thought about pulling away so he could see where he was going but his hand moved up the side of my body and I shivered kissing him harder. I could feel him laugh into my mouth. I started kissing his neck he groaned and pulled me closer. "I should make you suffer at least a little." He said into my neck

"Uh huh," I Said tracing his jaw with my tongue. "Your right I deserve it." I said as we fell onto the bed. I pulled away from him as soon as I heard the words come out of my mouth; he didn't seem to notice as he continued kissing my collar bone. A sudden electric surge went through me and it took all I had to not jump on top of him. "Brandon?" I said

"Ah huh," He had my shirt off now kissing around the outline of my bra and down to my stomach.

"Why aren't you?

"Why aren't I what babe?" he asked still focused on his mission. It was getting harder and harder to concentrate on what I wanted to say.

"Why aren't you making me suffer?" I started running my hands through his hair.

He stopped what he was doing, which immediately made me annoyed with myself. He propped himself up on his elbows and looked at me smiling sheepishly. "Because my love, when life finally makes you tall enough to reach the one thing you never thought you could have, you don't really want to waste any more time without it. You just sort of reach up and take it." He smiled at his own words and I laugh.

"So I'm like a cookie on top of the fridge when you're a little kid?" I ask giggling.

He laughed. "Yeah something like that," He said moving back up to kiss me again, his lips kissing

me more fiercely now. Hungry and I moaned and
pulled his shirt over his head running my hands
along his perfect chest. Every touch was like a
shock to me and I took a deep breath to take it all in.

CHAPTER TWENTY-THREE

When I woke up the sun was shining. I was awake but I didn't want to open my eyes because I was afraid it had all been a dream. "Please don't be a dream, please don't be a dream," I said out loud. I heard a deep chuckle beside me and I opened one eye. I immediately shot up in the bed, completely forgetting about my nakedness. He raised an eyebrow at me and smiled smugly. I realized my bareness and pulled the sheet over myself blushing and looking down. He laughed again. He moved this time leaning toward me. His hand caressed my face. If it wasn't for his intoxicating eyes I would not have been able to stop looking at his all too perfect body that he felt no need to hide under the covers. He kissed me and started to pull the sheet away from my body. I held onto for dear life turning redder and giggling.

"Come now Emma," he said warmly kissing my jaw and neck. "I like it so much better when I can see all of you. I have waited a very long time." He smiled mischievously and the sheet was gone replaced by his warm body. I giggled under him and he rolled over and looked at me with a huge grin on his face. "So tell me," he started, "is this as surreal for you as it is for me." He leaned over and kissed my collarbone.

"I would have to say that the last couple of weeks have been surreal, but this, this is the most real moment I have had." His grin was enormous when I said this and he kissed me again. Beside me the phone started ringing. "That's you sister." I said to him.

"Let her leave a message." He said and continued what he was doing. I giggled and didn't pick up. Then his phone started to ring. He chuckled. "She's persistent." He said but didn't move to answer it. When his phone stopped there was a loud knock at the door.

"She won't be ignored Brandon." I said doing my best impersonation of Glen Close from fatal attraction. He chuckled and finally released me. I jumped out of bed and threw on a pair of pant and a t-shirt and ran down stairs. When I opened the door she took in my appearance for a moment smiled and then pushed her way past me into the house. "Looking for something?" I said with a smirk and crossing my arms.

"Someone," She said with a grin and started walking toward the stairs.

I laughed, "I don't know who you could be referring to." She turned and rolled her eyes at me.

"How about the owner of that car out there?"

I laughed again, "oops."

"You look very happy." She said inspecting my
face. "Happy like I haven't seen you in years." My
smiled just grew wider. "Oh please tell what I think
happened, happened. Please tell me if I walk up
those stairs to your bed room I am going to find
who I think I am."

"Who do you think you're going to find?" Brandon
said coming down the stairs with a huge grin on his
face.

"Oh, oh, oh," She said getting more excited. Then
she stopped jumping and looked embarrassed.
"Oh." She said and laughed. "Should I leave?"

I giggled, "Could you?" Brandon said chuckling.

"No you're fine." I said walking over and smacking
him lightly on the arm. "Let me just go get
dressed." He looked down at me and frowned. I
laughed at him, "Hey you did." I said. He shrugged
his shoulders and kissed the top of my head and
smiled.

When I came back down stairs they were sitting at
the kitchen table. "So I would like to know what
finally made you realize." Allie said as I walked
into the room.

"Oh so would I." Brandon said and rested his chin on his hands and batted his eyes at me.

I laughed at both of them. "Last night, I looked at him, at you." I said turning to look at Brandon. He looked so handsome with his hair all messy sitting at my kitchen table. I giggled and he rolled his eyes and grinned. "And I realized that every hang up I've ever had about us was stupid and that I am totally and completely in love you with and I have been since I was eighteen."

He jumped up from his chair and kissed me. "Ok ewe seriously gross stop making out with my brother." But she was smiling at us.

"Aren't you going to ask him?" I said to her.

"No, I don't need to ask him. Why do you think I have been calling you an idiot for all these years?"

I pouted a little and Brandon chuckled. "I've been in love with you, since before I even knew what it felt like." He said to me. I smiled up at him, "it's been awful hard waiting twelve years for you to realize you felt the same."

"Ok so you've always known I was in love with you too. How am I the only person who didn't know this?"

He shook his head at me, "no, I didn't know, I just hoped," then kissed me again.

"Oh, wait, do I get to know what you and Michael fought about now? You both said it would cause me to pick a side. Can I know now, I sort of picked one." I said and snuggled into his side.

"I don't really think it's a good idea. Why do you have to know now? Does it really even matter?" he asked looking at me seriously.

I thought about it for a moment. "I think it does." I said.

He chuckled and Allie rolled her eyes. "He told me he wanted me to leave, go back to where ever I was and stay there."

"Why did he do that?" I asked him. I realized immediately that it was a stupid questions and I laughed at myself. "And what did you say?"

"I told him I wasn't going anywhere that I made the mistake of leaving once and I wasn't going to leave again. Then he basically said he would make you chose between us. So I pointed out to him that, that was a bad idea. That when someone forces you to choose you will always choose the latter. He realized I was right and said he would find a way without actually telling you, you had to choose. I said I would never make you make that decision.

You are a big girl and you can make your own mind up. If it turned out that he was really the one you were supposed to be with then I would be ok with that, all I have ever wanted is to just have you in my life."

"So you lied a little." I said laughing

He chuckled, "hey, I couldn't give him any fuel. Besides it isn't really a lie, I love being your best friend; I just prefer to be the best friend you want to make out with." He winked.

"So basically he tried to make you leave."

"Yes."

"Even though he knew it would break my heart."

"I'm not sure he really cared about what it would do to you, well maybe not that he didn't care but that he was more concerned about making sure he didn't lose you." Brandon said and Allie laughed.

"Yup sleeping with his secretary really helped with that." She said. Brandon glared at her.

"Look no one hates the guy as much as I do, trust me it isn't even possible, but he loved Emma. No matter what he is or what he did, in his own twisted way he loved you almost as much as I do." He smiled at me. I grinned back at him.

"And that was it? That was the whole fight that changed everything so completely." I asked.

He turned and looked at Allie, she just shrugged at him. "Thanks a lot." He said to her. "No Emma that wasn't the end of it. But I don't really want to talk about it now."

"Brandon please?" I pleaded.

"Why is this so important to you?" he asked unable to hide the annoyance in his tone.

"I can't really answer that to tell you the truth. It's just something I feel I need to know."

"And what if it changes things?" Allie asked.

"What?" I said looking at her strangely, as if what she had just said couldn't possibly be true.

"What if what happened after we had the fight changed the way you felt about things?"

"Not possible." I said. I was becoming more and more confused by the minute. "But when you say things like that it only makes me need to know more. Now please tell me."

"I never wanted to tell you any of this; I really don't see how it's relevant." He said.

"Brandon baby please." I pleaded again.

He looked down and then at Allie again who just shrugged, "You might as well explain what happened, you know she isn't going to let it go," she said to him.

He sighed, "Before he left my house, he turned back to me and said that whether you and I were meant to be together or not was beside the point. He said that you were far too sad and pathetic to ever have the strength to leave him. That deep down inside you wanted to be taken care of and you knew I could never do that. So he would find a way to get me and Allie out of your life, and then you wouldn't have anyone but him to lean on." I just stared at him shocked. He looked down again and then back up at me with those beautiful brown eyes of his and continued, "So I sort of lost it. When he walked out of the house I followed him with a bat and sort of took out the whole front end of his car. It was childish and stupid and I could have found a much better outlet for my anger but the things he said and… so I'm sorry."

"That was childish." I said to him

"I know." He said looking embarrassed

"Is that when he hit you?" I asked. He looked up at me shocked

"How did you…"

"Well about the same time his car was in the shop, you had the huge welt on your eye. I just figured he put it there."

"Yeah," He said

"And you pushed him or something?"

"Yes." He said looking at me with both shock and awe.

"Ok" I said and nodded, "good enough," And sat down on his lap. I wasn't completely ok with him having caused damage to both a vehicle and Michael but he had done it to defend me, for that I could over look his macho display.

"But I..."

"I don't really want to hear anymore. I have the feeling it didn't end there, and you're right, I should have just let it stay a secret."

"Are you angry with me?" he asked

I smiled at him and kissed him, "no, I'm not angry with you at all, but could you control the heroics from now on?"

"I think I can manage that." He said and kissed me back.

"This is weird." Allie said looking at the two of us.

I smiled at her then turned and kissed Brandon on the cheek, "Yeah it is."

He wrapped his arms around my waist and laughed, "I don't know, I kind of like it."

"I kind of feel like a tramp," I said to them.

"What? Why?" Allie said shocked.

"Um…because I just broke up with my fiancée like three days ago and already I'm…" I stopped and smiled at Brandon. "What am I?"

"Loved," He said and Allie and I groaned at him. He chuckled. "You're not a tramp Emm, you can't fight fate. But I guess, for lack of a better word you're my girlfriend."

I looked into his eyes and smiled. The way I felt about Brandon made the love I had for Michael feel like nothing more than I crush. It was good to finally have an explanation for why I got an electric charge every time he touched me, or why I always felt happier when he was around. I felt like I had, had blinders on for the last twelve years and I had finally taken them off. It felt so right, so comfortable. Like this really was what was supposed to happen and it had just taken a long time to figure it out. "You're beautiful." I said and kissed him.

"I love you Emma Grace." He whispered.

"I love you too Brandon Jacobs." I giggled. "You need a middle name."

He laughed, "I'll talk to my parents about that." He said. Allie cleared her throat and we both turned to look at her.

"Seriously, like to two of you weren't vomit inducing before this, I don't think I can stomach all the cute." She grinned as I moved to kick her. "Speaking of our parents, I think they might do back flips. Emma Grace Peter's loves their son, oh swoon!"

"Oh shut up." Brandon said with a chuckle. "Oh speaking of swooning, sorry we didn't get to meet Craig last night."

"I think dealing with Bob was more important. Besides, Emma is going to cook dinner for all of us tonight."

"I am?" I said laughing.

"Yup," She said. "It's payback, for years or having to deal with less than pleasant people."

"Ah." I said and nodded. "We have to go visit Bob today. I opened the present he gave me." I said to Brandon.

"Oh? What was it?" he asked

"Well, um… first he basically told me I was in love with you and that I was an idiot if I married his son." Brandon burst into laughter. "What's so funny?"

"You remember when you use to accuse Bob and me of having some scheme in the works?"

"Yeah," I said.

"He and Bob were trying to make you realize Michael wasn't right for you from the beginning. I don't think Bob realized that Brandon was the one you should have been with until about two months ago." Allie said

"How do you know this?"

"Margo told me." She answered with a shrug

"Wow everyone there really was out to get me." I said

"No, not out to get you. They just wanted to see you happy for a change." Brandon said. "But that couldn't have been the present. What was the present?"

"He's giving me the company." I said with a look of worry on my face. "What if he changes his mind now that Michael and I broke up? Plus I don't know if I can run that place. What if I mess up? What if I drive it into the ground? What if…" I was stopped by Brandon's lips on mine.

"Sorry, I thought it was the best way to make you shut up, Or at least the most fun for me." He grinned and his sister laughed beside us. "You deserve that company, you will be great. I'll help you, everyone will. And as for Bob, he isn't giving you the company because he thought you were going to marry his son. He is giving it to you because no one loves that place as much as he does, except you."

I smiled at him, "do you really think so?" I asked

"Absolutely," Allie said. "Oh I have to go." She said looking down at her watch." She got up from the table; "I will call you in a little while to let you know what time we will be here for dinner. Let me know how things go when you go to visit Bob. I love you, and I am so freaking happy I can't even stand myself right now." She laughed and kissed my cheek and then her brothers and ran out the door.

"Oh no we're all alone." He said trying to fight the grin forming at the corner of his lips.

"Oh no, whatever will we do with ourselves." I said with a giggle and with that he chased me up the stairs.

CHAPTER TWENTY-FOUR

A few hours later we were on our way to the hospital. I called Sophie when we were on the way. I didn't want to make things awkward if Michael was there visiting his father. I may love the man, but he was still his flesh and blood. Sophie let me know that the coast was clear and she was very excited, they both were, to talk to me.

When we got to the hospital Sophie met us at the elevator. She smiled widely at us as we got off the elevator. "Hello you two," She said

"Hello Sophie." I said and we took turns kissing her on the cheek.

She linked each of her arms around one of ours and walked towards Bob's room. She stopped just outside the door. "Brandon why don't you come with me to the cafeteria, I could really use a cup of coffee." She said smiling at him.

He nodded knowingly he stopped himself from kissing me. Sophie may have been ok with me not being with Michael and she knew Bob wanted Brandon and me to be together, but Michael was still her baby. "Of course," He said and the two of them left so I could talk to Bob alone.

I knocked on the door. "Come in kido." He said. He already sounded better than he had the previous night.

"Hey Bob, how are you feeling." I asked him.

"Well since my Sophie told me that you finally figured out what we were all talking about." I looked at him with a smile and blushed, I imagined that Michael had told her Brandon and I were together now. "I couldn't be happier Emma. You have the person you are meant to be with, and my son can find someone he is much more suited for."

I frowned a little, "I hope he does." I said. "I feel a bit guilty despite everything."

"Of course you do, that's your nature. You're a good person. But let's get down to business shall we. I assume you opened the present we are giving you?"

"Yes, Bob, that is too much just giving me the company like that."

"Emma I know that no one can take care of that place like you can. Do you know that until you started working for me I barely took a vacation? I didn't think anyone could handle it if I wasn't there. But then you came and it was like I was seeing the young female version of myself."

"But Bob, what about Michael?"

This made him chuckled. He winced a little. "Oh Emma, always so good. Do you really think that Michael would want to run the company? He barely thinks what we do is a job."

I smiled at him. He was absolutely right. "But how is he going to feel about you giving it to me, especially now."

"I don't really care how my son feels about it. He never showed any interest in it, and if he is worried about his inheritance, he shouldn't. He will be very well off when we finally go."

"I don't think he would be thinking that. I think he will just be trying to get back at me and you a little for wanting me to have it even now."

Bob grinned at me. "Why don't we worry about Michael when we need to? Let's just agree that I am giving you the company and there is nothing you can do to stop me." He smiled at me again and I had to laugh. "I am so happy about you and Brandon."

"You have to know that is a little bazaar for me." I said with a laugh.

He chuckled again "I imagine it would be. But I see the way you look at each other. He loves you more than I have ever seen anyone love a woman. He loves you like I love my Sophie. And you, you light up when his name is mentioned. The two of you were born to be together." He grinned pleased with himself.

"I do love him." I said

"I know." He said with a grin. "When I get out of here, we will all get together so we can finish all the paper work for you to take the company."

"Knock, knock." Sophie said as she walked in the room.

"Hello my love." Bob said to her as she walked into the room with Brandon right behind her. "Brandon my boy, how are you?" Bob said with a smile

"I got to tell you Bob, I'm pretty excellent." He said with a grin then winked at me. I laughed and rolled my eyes at him. "How are you feeling?"

"I've had better days. But, it's just confirmation that I am making the right decision to retire." He said

"Yes you are." Sophie said with a stern look on her face then smiled warmly at him as he took her hand.

"My Sophie always worried." He smiled at her. "So tell me my boy, what did you do to make this girl finally wake up and realized she loved you."

Brandon looked at him with a grin, "I don't think it was me that made her realize it, I think it was you. She kissed me after she read that letter you wrote."

"It was actually a combination of the two." I said to them. I was confused after I read the letter. It had been a very long day, no scratch that had been a very long week, but when he came over to see why I was crying, as soon as I looked at him it all made sense."

Brandon smiled down at me. "I'm glad you finally realized."

"Me too, I was starting to get on my own nerves." I said with a giggle and they all laughed. "I just wish things could have been different."

"How so?" Sophie asked.

"I don't know. I just feel…" I started but couldn't finish my thought.

"She feels like a tramp because she and Michael just broke up three days ago." Brandon answered for me. I just nodded.

Sophie laughed out loud, "Oh Emma honey, no one thinks that about you."

"I'm not so sure no one thinks that about me." I said with a frown. Brandon's face turned from happy to annoyed in two seconds. I could tell what he wanted to say, but considering the company he held his thoughts in.

"Who cares what he thinks." Bob said it for him. "Look he is my son, and I love him with all my heart, but at least you broke up with him before you went after someone else."

"Bob, How did… How did you know that he…?"

"Emma my dear, I could see it on his face when he was here last night. We talked about the fact that the two of you broke up and I could tell that it was over for good. Neither of you had to tell me what happened. The little chippy that kept calling him while he was here was enough proof for me of what he did. So you shouldn't feel like a tramp at all. You're with the right person now, and my son will… well my son will pretty much do whatever he wants now wont he."

I smiled at Bob. I was sad for him. I was sad for Michael too that he couldn't seem to appreciate anyone who loved him. Maybe if he could have, things would be different. I turned and look at Brandon. His beautiful brown eyes sparkled at me and his smiled made me want to kiss him, no things definitely would not have been different; it just may have been a harder choice.

We visited with Bob and Sophie for about an hour longer. We made plans to meet when Bob was out of the hospital with our lawyers to finalize my taking over the company. Bob thought that everything would move along smoothly, I, however, had my doubts.

CHAPTER TWENTY-FIVE

"Ok so where did she meet this guy again,"
Brandon asked me as we were waiting for Allie and
Craig to come over.

I rolled my eyes at him, "do you ever pay attention
when other men are mentioned."

"I pay attention when you mention them." He said
with a chuckled.

I giggled and slapped him playfully. "He's a chef.
They met when she was looking for a caterer for a
party. So great I get to cook for a chef." I said and
made a face.

He chuckled again. "You're a great cook. I am sure
he will just be happy he didn't have to make it.
You know Allie never cooks for him."

I laughed, "Would you want Allie to cook for him?
I am sure she's baked something for him though,
that she can do."

"Mmm yes she can." He patted his belly. "I am glad
she met someone she likes."

I smiled widely, "me too, I want my Al to be as
happy as I am." I turned from the stove and

wrapped my arms around his waist. "I really do love you."

"I really do love you right back." I leaned down and kissed me. I smiled up at him and blushed.

"Am I interrupting something again?" Allie said as she walked into the kitchen. The two of us jumped and she giggled. "Oh sorry, did I scare you?"

"Wow! Yes, how did you get in here without us hearing you at all?" I said

She shrugged, "I'm stealth." She said with a grin. "What's for dinner?"

"Emma's making dinner, what do you think it is?" Brandon said and moved away before I could hit him.

"Oh I like chicken parm." She said and came over to kiss my cheek. "You want to come out and meet him?" she asked with an anxious look on her face.

"Honey, are you nervous?" I asked her smiling.

"I am." She blushed. "I really want you guys to like him. There is nothing worse than having the people you love hate the person you're dating."

"I wouldn't know anything about that." I said and we all laughed.

"I heard all kinds of fun going on in here, I had to come and check it out." A man walked into my kitchen that I had to assume was Craig.

I smiled at him, "you must be Craig." I said and put my hand out to shake his.

"You must be Emma, I have heard a lot about you." He smiled.

"I'm sure it was all good." I laughed. "This is Brandon, Allie's brother."

"Nice to meet you" Brandon said shaking his hand.

"I've heard a lot about you too, all good." Craig said smiling "I promise." Allie beamed at him. "So you too are together right?" he said motioning between Brandon and me.

I blushed, "yes it s recent development." Brandon answered him.

"I heard that, but the way your sister talks I thought the two of you had been together for years," he grinned at me.

"Should have been," Allie said. "Ok what can I do?"

"You can go open the wine and then sit down, everything is just about ready." I said and started to shoo them all out of the kitchen. Brandon started to follow them and I grabbed him by the back of the shirt.

"I thought I got to be a guest too?" I pulled him from the collar of his shirt and kissed him. "Oh." He said and grinned picking me up and kissing me again. When he put me down I reached over and grabbed the bowl of pasta and handed it to him. "Ah you're just using me." He said with a laugh.

"Buttering you up to be my slave," I grinned

"Oh?" he said raising his eyebrow at me.

I laughed, "You're a perv. Come on lets go eat."

I watched Craig through most of dinner. He was funny and he kept touching Allie in small ways. He would touch her hand or her arm. He pushed the hair from her face a couple of times. He was great. He was funny and smart and he had just enough attitude to deal with Allie. I think any one on the outside would be sick at the sight they saw. As if one couple in the honeymoon stage wasn't gross enough, we had two. Brandon held my hand as much as he could that would allow us to still eat. It had to be one of the most pleasant dinner's I had, had in a really long time. It was nice being around people I liked and that I had things in common with. When dinner was over we went and sat in the living room.

"So when did the two of you start dating?" Craig asked us

Brandon laughed, "Um... like two am."

"This morning?"

"Yup," Brandon turned and grinned at me, he had is arm wrapped around my shoulder.

"Yeah, it seems that Emma just came to her senses this morning." Allie said with a smile.

"Wow! You two seem like you've been together forever. I don't think I have seen to people who fit together so seamlessly. I'm impressed." He smiled and nodded.

"I think that's a product of us being best friends for so long." I said

Craig shook his head slightly, "no I think its fate. I don't know you very well, but it seems pretty obvious to me."

Brandon smiled at him, "that's what I've been trying to tell her."

I rolled my eyes at the two of them and looked at Allie. She just looked at me with a smiled and shrugged. "It's true." She said.

I just shook my head at them, "whatever." I said with a smile. "Who wants dessert?"

"Oh me please," Brandon said

I got up from the couch to go into the kitchen, "I'll help." Allie said. I turned and smiled at her as we walking into the kitchen. "So what do you think?"

"He's lovely" I said squeezing her hand.

"You really think so." She said with and anxious smile

"Would I lie to you?"

She looked at my face carefully, "um…"

"Allie please, After all the aggravation you gave me about Michael you think that I would lie to you about whether or not I liked someone you were dating."

She thought for a minute, "No I think you would tell me you hate his guts if you hated his guts."

"Exactly," I said with a smile. I poked my head out of the doorway to look at the two men in the living room. "Your brother seems to like him. That's always a good sign."

She put her hand on my shoulder and looked over my head. When she stood up straight again she had a smiled on her face. "They seem to like one another."

I laughed, "Yes honey they do. I've never seen you like this."

"Emma he's lovely. He's so smart and funny and he thinks I'm funny. No one thinks I'm funny."

"I think you're funny."

"You don't count; you have to think I'm funny." I laughed at her. "And his schedule is as crazy as mine, but we seem to have all the same time off and…" she just stopped and grinned.

"I'm so happy for you Allie." I hugged her.

"I'm so happy for you too. It's about time."

"You could have told me you know."

"No I couldn't have. You wouldn't have believed me. 'No sir, Brandon and I are just friends there is totally no tension between us because we are both madly in love with each other and refuse to admit it to ourselves.'"

"Oh shut up." I said with a giggle.

"See you know I am right. I am just glad you figured it out before you married Michael."

"I don't think I was ever going to marry Michael. Especially with how much he changed after Brandon came home."

"Jealousy will do that to you."

I frowned at her. "I am still really annoyed with your brother for leaving all those years."

She smiled, "he kicked himself everyday for not taking you with him."

"Really?"

"Yes of course really. That boy loves you with everything he has. He left because he thought you would never feel the same."

"And I'm the idiot?" she laughed, "ok, we should bring them out some dessert before they think we are talking about them."

"We are." She laughed.

"Yes but if they know that they might get big heads," We laughed and took the dessert into the living room. The four of us ate and talked some more. Craig really was a super nice guy. When they were gone Brandon turned to me.

"I like him." He said with a big grin. "He's good for her."

"I agree." I said.

We went and sat down on the couch. "Emma, I'm sorry."

"For what? What could you possibly be sorry for?"

"I should have asked you to come with me when I left. Or I at least should have come home sooner."

I nodded. "You should have, either of those you should have done. But I should have just come after you, or asked you to come home. But I was too blind to see that, that's what I wanted."

"I never meant to hurt you Emma."

I smiled at him, "Brandon honey, I didn't even realize it hurt until a few days ago. Before I thought it was just me missing you. I also thought that I loved you just as a friend until recently, so basically I have been completely in the dark about my own feelings so don't apologize for hurting me. You can't be sorry for something I didn't even know was happening."

"You're confusing sometimes." He chuckled.

"You should be inside my head. It's way worse." I giggled and he kissed me.

"I am the luckiest guy in the whole world. I finally feel like a whole person." I giggled and he kissed me. "Oh, so remember when you said your life was almost perfect."

"Yeah," I said smiling

"And you couldn't put your finger on what it was that was missing."

"Yeah," I said my smiled widening.

"Can you put your finger on it yet?" he asked with a grin. I laughed and reached out and touch his arm with my finger. He chuckled, "Dork."

I shrugged, "that's why you love me." I said and kissed him.

"It all just seems too simple."

"Were you expecting it to be hard?"

"In my experience with love, it's never easy."

"That's because it's never been with the right person. In my own experience, as much as I thought I had been in love before. As much as I had been in love before, the love I had for those men is nothing compared to how I feel about you." And with that the conversation was over as he kissed me.

About a month later we were sitting on the couch reading the Sunday paper. Things had been going well all around. Allie and Craig were very happy. Brandon had barely left my house except to get clothes. Work was going well. Most of the people in the office had taken him and me dating very well. None as well, of course, as Margo who was beside herself and couldn't wait to tell me she knew it all along. Bob had come home from the hospital and I was set to meet with him and his lawyers that afternoon. George of course would be coming with me; he had looked over the papers Bob had given me to make sure that everything seemed ok. Everything was going smoothly.

"Hey." I said to him, pushing him lightly with my foot.

"Hmm," He said smiling but not looking up from the sports page.

"Why don't you just stay here?" I said as nonchalantly as I could.

His smile widened. "What do you mean?" he asked trying to fight off the chuckle that so obviously wanted to escape his lips. "I already am staying here."

"You know what I mean Brandon."

"No Emma, I haven't the slightest idea what you mean."

"You're going to make me say it aren't you?"

"I am" he said now unable to fight off the chuckle. "I would like very much if you asked me."

"Would you want to?"

"Would I want to what?"

"GAH! You're infuriating." He put down the paper and looked at me with one eyebrow raised. "You're so cute when you do that."

He burst into a fit of laughter. "Stop changing the subject and just ask."

"Why are you making me ask, if you already know the question? Do you enjoy torturing me?"

He thought about it for a minute, "I think I do." He said with that boyish grin I loved so much.

I rolled my eyes at him. "I love you."

"I love you too." He said looking at me expectantly.

"Oh fine." I said giving up, "Brandon would you like to move in with me."

He grinned at me, "but it's so soon." He chuckled.

"Gah!" I said and went to get up from the couch.

He pulled me back to him and wrapped his arms around me so I couldn't get away. "Of course I want to move in with you silly girl." And then he kissed me. "Now finish reading your paper we have to leave to meet Bob in a little while."

I smiled at him. "Good." I said and went back to reading the paper.

"Emma." He said

"Yeah?"

"This is really happening right? I'm not going to wake up tomorrow and you're still going to be with Michael and I will have missed my chance right?" I grinned at him and pinched his arm. "Ouch!" he said with a smirk.

"Nope you're awake, it's not a dream." I giggled as he dived across the couch and tackled me. "I'm never going to get to finish my paper." I said.

"Your paper will still be here when we come home tonight." He said and he kissed me. I giggled and threw the paper up in the air.

CHAPTER TWENTY-SIX

A few hours later we were standing on Bob and Sophie's front stoop. "Hello you two," Sophie said as she opened to door. She had a worried look on her face.

"Sophie what's the matter? Is Bob ok?" I asked.

"Oh yes sweetie Bob is fine it…"

Bob came walking around the corner before she finished. "Hey there," He said with the same worried smile.

"What's going on Bob?" Brandon asked him.

"I'm so sorry." He said as we walked into the dining room where everyone was waiting. Sitting at the head of the table was Michael.

I took a deep breath. "I expected this." I whispered to Bob.

"I'm sorry Kido, I didn't" I smiled at him and patted his arm as I sat at the table.

"Hello Michael." I said without any coldness behind it, I even surprised myself.

"Emma," he said with a faint sad smile. "Brandon." He almost spat.

"Michael" he said with all the coldness that was absent from my greeting. He sat down beside me but was a good enough man to not hold my hand or touch me in any way. Something I am sure Michael wouldn't have done had the roles been reversed.

George was seated on my other side. He was already waiting when we got there. "So shall we get started then?" He asked looking around the room.

"Yes please." Bob said. "I would like Emma to take over the business. She is the only person who loves it as much as I do and I want her to be the one to take my place."

"You can't just give the company to her." Michael said.

"I can son; it's my company to give."

"But I'm your son you didn't even think to ask if I wanted it."

Bob chuckled at this. "Michael you don't even think what we do is work. Why would you want to take over the company? And it better be a better reason then you just don't want Emma to have it."

"That's not it at all." He said coldly, "it would have been nice if you asked. And why are you just giving it to her, you could at least sell it to her. She should have to pay something she isn't you flesh and blood."

"Sometimes it feels like she is." Bob spat back.

I sat and watched the exchange between the two of them becoming more and more annoyed. I looked at Sophie's face and she looked like she wanted to cry as she watched her son and her husband fighting. I couldn't bear the thought that I was the cause. "Enough." I said and they all looked at me. "That's enough."

"Why don't you just stay out of this?" Michael said coldly.

"Oh I don't know Michael maybe it's because you're discussing my future as well and I think I have a right to an opinion on that."

He snickered, "you should have to buy it." He said

"That's enough Michael; if you like I will sell it to her for one hundred dollars."

Michael just stared at him, "are you mocking me." He said.

"What do you think is a fair price Michael?" Brandon asked. "What do you think the fair price for the woman who put up with you for two years and spent eight years helping your father build up his business to what it has become is?"

Michael glared at him. "Yes Michael what would you like me to pay. If it makes you happy I can always give the money to you." I said.

Michael snickered again. "You couldn't afford it." He said

"Give me a price Michael."

"No bank will give you a loan for it. You're insane if you think you can buy it."

"A price Michael," I said glaring at him now.

"One point five million," He said with a smirk then leaned back in his chair crossing his arms.

"Michael that is outrageous" Sophie said. "You can't ask her to pay that. Where is she going to get that kind of money?"

His smirk grew wider and he snickered again. "Maybe I don't want her to have it." He said. "It's my father's business I have the right to stake a claim."

I looked at George who smiled and nodded,
"Done." I said.

They all turned and looked at me and Brandon
chuckled. "Excuse me?" Michael said.

"One point five million seems like a reasonable
amount of money. Would you like me to wire it to
you or would you like a check?" I smiled at him.
The most evil, condescending grin I could muster.

He laughed again, "And where are you going to
come up with that kind of money. You don't make
enough to pay back a loan like that."

"You're and idiot Michael." I said

"What?" he said coldly.

"She's rich you moron." Brandon said.

"She's what?"

"Did you think when my parents died they left me
with nothing? I don't touch the money because it
only reminds me of how I got it. But I think they
would be happy if I used some of it to buy
something that made me happy."

"Some of it? What do you mean some of it? How
much money do you have, and how does he know
you have it and I didn't?"

"He knows because he was with me when I got it. And I actually have no idea how much money I have." I turned and looked at George.

He smiled, "the last time I checked Emma is worth about nine and a half million give or take a few."

"I can't believe you never told me." Michael said coldly.

"Like she said she doesn't like to think about it. The only thing she has ever used any of it for it to buy her house." Brandon took my hand then.

"So do we have a deal Michael? Will you stop interfering in my taking over the company if I pay you what you asked?"

He couldn't speak he just stared at me, and then nodded. Bob smirked at me, "Ok then." And we continued with all the paperwork. A short time later Michael simply got up and left. "Well that was unexpected." Bob said to me.

"Which part?" I said with a smile.

"That you have been living on the pithily little salary I have been giving you." He chuckled and Sophie smiled.

I just smiled at him, "I love my job Bob, why do you think I am willing to pay off your son."

At the end of the day Brandon and I said good-bye to Bob and Sophie. George had left to get the check ready for me to bring to Michael the next day. Brandon turned to me when we were in the car. "That was a very expensive break up." He said with a chuckle.

I smiled at him and smacked his arm lightly. "It's easier this way. Now I don't have to feel guilty, like I got something for nothing."

"You have nothing to feel guilty about Emma, you didn't ask Bob to give you the company he wanted to."

I shrugged, "still."

He laughed at me, "you're such an interesting creature Emma, you feel guilty for standing up for yourself and being given things you clearly deserve." He shook his head.

I just smiled at him, "I can't wait to tell your sister."

"Oh she is going to be so mad she missed the look on his face when you said deal." He turned and looked at me, "I know I would be if I had missed it."

"You got a lot of joy out of today didn't you?" I laughed. "I don't like the fact that I hurt him you know. He isn't all bad; he was a good man for a long time. He just wasn't the right guy for me."

He grinned, "Nope, cause that's me." I shook my head at him and laughed.

"Then what happened?" Allie said as she sat across the table from me and I told her about my day. Craig sat beside her laughing at her enthusiasm. She turned and looked at him, "you don't understand babe, this guy put my best friend through the ringer, he talked down to her, made her feel bad about herself, tried to make my brother leave town and then cheated on her, my joy in his pain is simply vindication."

Now I was laughing at her, "She's not evil." I said to Craig with a smile, "but she is vindictive so be careful." He chuckled.

She rolled her eyes at the two of us, "Ok, ok so then what?"

Brandon came into the room from the kitchen with some coffee. "Then she told him she was loaded, offered him the money in a check or a wire transfer and that was pretty much that. Oh and she asked me to move in with her."

"It sounds like you had a very busy day." Craig said with a smile.

"I did." I said, and then laughed.

"I wish I could have seen his face when you told him you would give him the money."

"I told you she would say that." Brandon said looking at me.

"I could have told you she would say that." Craig said laughing.

"Ok people stop picking on me." Allie said with a fake pout.

"See now you know how I have felt for the last twelve years." I said with a smirk.

She smiled at me and kicked me under the table. "I think that everything is going to be great now. Can't you feel it? It feels like things are falling into place."

Brandon smiled at her, "I can actually, and I am hoping that soon even more things are going to change for the better." Then the two of them smiled at one another.

"I so hate when the two of you do that." I said to them

"What are they doing?" Craig asked looking between them.

"They have this secret smile when they are up to something, like some psychic sibling connection. They do it all the time and I always have to wait for it to happen."

"Diabolical." He said and laughed. "You and I should start telling each other secrets and keep it from them."

"I like the way you think Mr. Prestly." I smiled, "Craig's my new best friend so there." I said and stuck my tongue out at them.

Brandon rolled his eyes. "Why don't we ever tell you?" he said

"Because you're usually talking about me."

"And what do you love?"

"You," I said and giggled.

He chuckled, "I love you too, but you know what I mean."

"Surprises," I said defeated.

"Alright then, shut up." Allie said. "And besides if he tells you a secret about me I expect you to tell me." She said to me and motioned to Craig.

"Nope can't do it, I can't betray my new best friend." I laughed and dodged the cookie she threw at me.

"So when are you taking him the check?" Craig asked

"George said he would have it ready by tomorrow, so I guess I will take it to him then, to get it over with."

"Tomorrow!!" Allie asked then tried to look at her brother without me noticing.

Brandon laughed, "Yeah she should have it tomorrow morning, we will be taking it over in the afternoon."

"Ah." Allie said then smiled.

"You want us to come with you?" Craig asked.

"Moral support, good thinking babe," Allie said and kissed him.

He chuckled, "I do what I can." And then they both looked at Brandon then me.

"If you really want to come that's fine, but could you stay in the car. I think it will be hard enough with him there." I said motioning to Brandon.

"Can do," Allie said. "Then you know what I think we should do?" Allie said and then looked at Brandon. He gave her a dirty look, and then she stuck her tongue out at him.

"Alright knock it off the two of you."

"You will tell me what this is all about on the way back to your house right?" Craig asked Allie. She smiled and nodded at him.

"Betrayal," I yelled at him and laughed.

"Sorry buddy, but I have to know." He smiled sympathetically. "What do you think we should do after that?" he turned back to Allie and asked her.

She grinned at her brother, "We should go to the red sox game."

"You suck Allison." Brandon said to her.

"Is that my surprise? You only call her that when she does something that makes you mad." I asked excited.

They looked at each other and smiled. "Sure is babe." He said in a way that I knew was a lie.

"Gah," I said, "Forget it I can wait. I am clearly a patient woman," I said and stuck my tongue out at Brandon.

He laughed, "You're not nearly as patient as I am." He said and winked at me.

When Allie and Craig left I turned and walked over to Brandon who was sitting on the couch. "Can you please tell me?" I said to him while batting my eyelashes.

He chuckled, "Nope sorry, trust me you are going to be happy I waited."

I sat on his lap and kissed him neck, "please." He groaned and shook his head. I moved and kissed the other side of his neck, "please."

"Emma Grace, I will not tell you what is going on. Now please stop asking or I will sleep on the couch." He pulled away from me and looked at my face. There was a smile threatening at his lips. "Seriously please Emma; I need you to just stop asking. I have a really hard time not giving you what you want, and I know you will be really mad at yourself if you make me tell you."

I sat back on the couch and pouted. "Fine," I said and crossed my arms across my chest. I smile was starting to threaten the corners of my mouth as well.

"Good." He said and kissed me. "Come on we have a long day tomorrow, let's get to bed," and with that he threw me over his shoulder and walked upstairs.

CHAPTER TWENTY-SEVEN

The next morning we went to George's office to pick up the check. "Are you sure this is what you want kid?" he asked me.

"George, there have been few things in my life I have been this sure of. The other is sitting out in the waiting room."

He smiled at me, "Your dad would be really proud of the woman you've become. He would like that you're using your money for something that makes you so happy. He would like that you're finally with Brandon too. He liked that kid; he always thought the two of you would end up together."

"Really?" I asked him, unable to hide the tears forming in my eyes.

"Yeah, he really did. Now go give this check to that jackass and let me know how it goes. You're a good kid Emma, I'm glad I get to know you."

"You're a good man George, thanks for taking such good care of me all these years. I am sure my Dad is grateful where ever he is."

"Thanks kid. Now get out of here before you make me cry like a sissy." I smiled and kissed him on the cheek before leaving his office.

"You ready beautiful?" Brandon asked with a smile.

"As I will ever be to part with this much money," I said laughing as we walked to the car.

We went and picked up Allie and Craig then drove to Michael's office. I took a deep breath before getting out of the car. Brandon squeezed my hand. "I can take it to him if you want me to." He said

"Nope, I've got this. Let's go."

"Good luck." Craig and Allie both said.

When we walked off the elevator people started staring at us. Dawn looked up from her desk and half smiled. I just looked at her as I walked through Michael's office door. I turned and looked at Brandon. "Stay here ok." I said to him

"Are you sure?" he asked, concern covering his face.

"Very." I said. He leaned over and kissed me and I walked into Michael's office. "Hello Michael." I said

"Emma." He said turning to look at me.

I took the check from my pocket. "Here you go." I said putting it on his desk. "Now you have your money and I have the company.

"Great." He said and looked away.

"So this is really how we are going to end this." I said to him. "After all this time you are just going to end it with a great and me walking out the door."

"How else would you like me to end it Emma, what would you like me to say." I just looked at him. He sighed. "I'm sorry." He said and I knew it was for more than simply not having something better to say. I nodded. "This is hard for me you know. Way harder than I thought it would be."

"Yeah I know. I'll go." And I turned to walk out the door.

"Your face used to light up whenever you talked about him, you know?" Michael said

I turned and looked at him. "What?"

"Brandon, whenever you talked about him your whole face would light up. It was a smile I never saw for me. You could light up a room with it. But I knew you didn't realize you were in love with him, and I hoped he wasn't in love with you. But

320

either way I knew if he stayed away it didn't matter. You would never realize you loved him and I would never have to lose you. Kind of a dick thing to do isn't it." He said with a tiny smile. "I didn't want to lose you, I love you Emma, you're the best thing that ever happened to me and I thought I could make you happy. I knew you would never love me like you loved him, but I was ok with that. It was something I could live with."

"Michael…" I started as I stared at him in shock.

"Please Emm let me just say this. It's a whole bunch of things I should have said that I was too much of a jerk to say. I was never good enough for you, but I thought I could be… adequate. I mean if this guy could leave you for all those years surely he couldn't possibly be in love with you, not like he should be, so I convinced myself that I deserved you and he was a fool. Then he came home and the light you use to get when you talked about him only intensified. And I saw, when he looked at you that he loved you more than I had ever seen anyone love another person, except the way you loved him. But you still didn't know. So I thought I could keep it that way, I thought I could convince you that I was the person for you. So I became the perfect boyfriend. But I couldn't keep it up; no matter how good I was I knew that he was the person you were supposed to be with. So I started to try and make you see that, because I knew I didn't have the strength to simply walk away." He paused and took a breath. I had sat down in the chair across from his desk taking in the information he was now thrusting at me. "But I made one last attempt to keep you for myself, to test how much he loved you. I asked him to leave. I told him I would make you choose."

"He told me." I said scowling.

He chuckled, "I thought he might."

"He did defend you though."

"I thought he might do that as well. He's a good guy that Brandon. But he said something I wasn't expecting. I expected him to fight back, that's what I would have done. But instead he said that he wasn't going to leave, but if I really was the right person for you he would be ok with that, he wanted you to be happy and that was all that mattered. It hurt and I pushed his buttons a little more than I should have. My front bumper paid the price for that." He stopped and smiled at me.

"So I made the decision, you had to be with him." He motioned to the door. "I never slept with Dawn, well not until the night my father had the heart attach and you came to get your things. When I heard the things I said to you I knew it was over, I knew it was only a matter of time before you came back and told me it was. So I called her. You were right she is the same girl that was my first kiss. We have been friends since elementary school. So I asked her to do me the favor of pretending she was my mistress and that we had been sleeping together the whole time Brandon had been home. I wanted to make it easier for you to walk away. I know you better than you think I do, I knew you would feel guilty for wanting to be with him more than me unless I gave you a damn good reason to think otherwise."

My mouth had fallen open by now and he smiled at me. "Michael, I had…"

"You weren't supposed to have any idea Emma. It was easier if you just thought I was a complete prick. You are with the right person now."

"And you?"

"I think maybe I am too." He said with a smile towards the door.

"Why are you telling me this now?"

"I don't want this money Emma; I just wanted to see if you would just give up. I have to tell you though, you having the money to begin with was a huge shocker, and how did you hide this from me for so long."

I smiled, "I wasn't hiding it, I just don't like to think about it."

He nodded, "I am truly happy for you Emma, you are an amazing and beautiful person and I never deserved you, I am so sorry I was so selfish for so long so you couldn't figure out who you loved sooner."

"I did love you Michael. I still do in many ways"

He smiled, "I know you do. I never doubted you loved me. That's why I held out hope that you would pick me, but I know that was unfair. I love you Emma, more than I have ever loved anyone. I just hope the next time I find it, I won't mess it up."

"Or she won't be in love with someone else and not know it." I said with a giggle. He laughed and placed his hand on his heart like I had just stabbed him.

"Good luck Emma and I will make sure that everything goes smoothly with you taking over the company."

"Thank you Michael and I hope you find the happiness you are looking for."

"And I hope that boy gives you everything you deserve, or I'm coming to take him out."

324

I smiled and walked over to hug him. "I'm glad you told me this. I didn't want to go through life hating you, not when I had loved you so much."

"And I don't want you to hate Me." he hugged me tightly. "Thank you for being part of my life Emma, you are more extraordinary than you could ever realize."

"Thank you lovely Michael." He chuckled and pulled away. "Good bye"

"I am sure I will see you around, I expect an invite to the wedding." I laughed and we said one last goodbye as I left his office.

CHAPTER TWENTY-EIGHT

When I walked outside Brandon and Dawn were both standing there "I'm sorry," I said to her.

She shrugged, "If the roles had been reversed and I thought you had been sleeping with my man for five months, I would not have been so civil."

I laughed and smiled at her. "How long have you been standing there?" I turned and asked Brandon.

"Long enough to hear a pretty good story," He smiled down at me. "Are you ready to go?"

"Yes I think I am." I said and we walked to the elevator and out of Michael's building.

"So do you think we should tell Allie what he said?" Brandon asked me in the elevator.

I turned and looked at him, "I think I'm still processing what he said."

"I told you he loved you in his own little way."

I looked up at him and he smiled his big goofy grin down at me, "I love you so much." I said to him. "You have been the most amazing man to me as long as I have known you. And sometimes I think, someone messed up somewhere because there is no

326

way that I deserve you." he took me into his arms and kissed me.

"Emma Grace, I love you more than I thought it was possible to love someone."

I smiled, "good." I said and we walked out of the elevator to the car. When we got to it, Allie and Craig were making out in the back seat. I knocked on the window. "Excuse me kids, do your parents know where you are?"

Craig chuckled and Allie let out a loud giggle. "Sorry." She said, "I couldn't help myself."

"That's ok Emma made out with me in the elevator." Brandon said and opened the passenger side door for me.

I laughed and shrugged. "So how did it go?" Craig asked straightening out his shirt and laughing at Allie's hair which was standing straight up.

"What?" she asked. I laughed and reach back to smooth it out. She giggled, "Oh."

"It went well, he gave the check back." I said.

"He what?" Allie asked

"Yeah he gave it back. I am still processing what happened, but in a nut shell, he isn't as much of a jerk as we thought."

"Not possible," she said shaking her head.

"No it's true." Brandon said, "He had a messed up way of doing it, but he actually did a stand up kind of thing. He never cheated on Emma; he just made her think he did so she wouldn't feel guilty when she finally realized she was in love with me."

"Aw come on, I want to hate him, don't tell me this."

I laughed, "well deal with it, I have to." And with that we were off to the game.

When we got to the park we took a familiar route to behind home plate. When we stopped to take out seats I looked up at Brandon and almost cried. "Did you call George?" I asked him.

"I may have," he grinned. The seats he had for the game belonged to the man my father worked with. They were the same seats my family and I used to sit in.

When we sat down an attendant came over and handed us all beer and hotdogs. "Wow what service, how did you manage this?" I asked.

Allie turned and looked at Craig, "I called in a few favors." He said and smiled.

"Keep him, don't ever let him get away," I said and we all laughed. It was a great game. We had a few beers and some hot dogs to celebrate my becoming a business owner. Around the seventh inning stretch Allie squealed. "What?" I said looking at her. She pointed to the outfield. I turned and looked at the screen in center field and then quickly at Brandon who was now on his knee in front of me. On the screen it said

Emma Grace will you marry me?

I stared at him as he opened to ring box and looked at me. I could feel all the eyes around us staring at me, waiting for my answer. "I bought the ring you always wanted, and I asked my parents' permission." He stopped and looked at me. I was still stunned and Allie kicked me. But Brandon just smiled and said, "Well? Will you marry me Emma Grace?"

I could feel the tears streaming down my face. The ring was beautiful. It was a three stone, white gold ring with princess cut diamonds. It was perfect, the exact ring I had always dreamed about. I knew Allie had a little to do with it. It was finally the right ring, in the right place with the right guy. I smiled at him, "it took you long enough to ask." I said and kissed him. A cheer sprang up around us as he lifted me into the air. "Of course I'll marry you. Of course, of course, of course!!" I said into his ear,

"So that's a maybe?" he said with a chuckle then kissed me.

"Well Jesus it's about freaking time. Can we watch the game now?" Allie said trying to be nonchalant but then leaped up and wrapped her arms around me. "Yay! She shouted. "Now this wedding I can't wait to be the maid of honor for."

"Congrats." Craig said with a smile.

So I guess that pretty much brings us up to date. I took over the company smoothly. Bob retired and took Sophie on a tour around the world. They sent me post cards from all over. They came home just for the wedding then took off again. Bob promised her he would show her the world when he married her, she was forcing him to make good on his promise now.

Michael and Dawn are together. She quit her job as his assistant and got a job somewhere else. I think that was smart, I wouldn't have wanted Michael to be my boss when we were dating either. Brandon is fine with his wife being his boss though. There are some times he likes it a little bit more, but that's not something we need to get into. Michael is happy, and I am happy for him. We talk every so often. He came to the reception. But he said he couldn't come to the ceremony. "As happy as I am for you, and as much as I love Dawn, that is something I don't know if I can handle." I respected that. I am sure if the roles were reversed I would have felt the same way.

Allie and Craig moved into together shortly after Brandon and I got engaged. Allie doesn't know it, but he is going to propose in a couple of weeks. Now I get to be the maid of honor.

The wedding was amazing, Allie and Craig made sure of it. It was a nice quiet clambake in Cape Cod. There were only about sixty people there and I cried as I walked towards Brandon standing there waiting for me. His father gave me away, a sentiment both a bit strange and completely perfect at the same time.

And as for the two of us now, it's been eight months since the wedding and we are expecting a baby girl in three months. I would say that things turned out even more perfect then I could have imagined. There is one thing for sure; we will have one hell of a story to tell our kids some day.

Made in the USA
Charleston, SC
26 February 2013